THE ANANDA ACCORDS

Ezekiel Springer Jr.

Editor: Matthew Cox

Book Cover by Andrijus Guscia of Rocking Book Covers

First edition [2022]

ISBN 979-8-9873763-1-7

This book is dedicated to my wife, Rochell,
and to the members of my writing group,
The Climbing Ivies of Blackrock,
Justine, Soyam, Kevin, Gabe, and Randyn.

The Ananda Accords

By

Ezekiel Springer Jr.

Chapter One

There it is again. Another wave of turbulence rocks our shuttlecraft as we descend to the planet, Sunder. Our transport loudly vibrates from side to side in its controlled drop. A bit of old-school roller-coaster dips and hops are thrown in just to shake things up; no pun intended. My insides rattle against my ribcage, so I grab my armrests in a futile attempt to steady myself. I hope I can at least keep breakfast down.

Since we've been shaking like a flying maraca for the last fifteen minutes, you'd think the pilot would get on the intercom and announce to us civilians that this flight has hit a patch of bad upper atmosphere. But this is a military VIP shuttle. They're used to being shot at; turbulence is nothing in comparison. One of the soldiers, an expressionless major, returns from the cockpit and takes his seat with no news at all. I guess bravado, honor, and duty demand these soldiers refrain from complaining about a little old thing like turbulence.

To top things off, a migraine headache declares itself inside my skull. First, it arrives as a pinprick in the back of my head, next as a shot behind my eye. Like an exploding sunburst, the migraine takes the shuttlecraft's artificial light and amplifies it tenfold. Everything and everyone inside the cabin become awash in a veneer of pure white light I can only stand for a few seconds. I shut my eyes tight. Despite all of Earth's technological advancements, migraines still suck.

Checking my blazer pocket and briefcase for pharmacological relief, I contemplate the possible source of my migraine. Typically, it's bright flashing lights or construction noise, stress even. This damn turbulence could be considered stressful, but no, that's not it. Currently, the source of my intensifying headache is seated directly across the aisle from me: General Rheinhold Alvarez, of the Earth Expeditionary Force, or EEF. My ability to remain cordial toward him on this diplomatic mission has worn thin.

While sitting cross-legged and statue-still, courtesy of his expert military training, Alvarez turns to me, in a deliberate manner, keeping his uniform cap respectfully nestled in his lap. "If you ask me, Ambassador Dylan..." Alvarez always starts in on me with a swagger that can only come from years being in command. "The only thing those ditch-digging, nitrous-breathing Adamahn know is the sword, so I say we should continue to oblige the bastards!"

As I pop a pain pill, Alvarez shoots me this toothsome grin. His eyes are antsy, but not from the turbulence we experience. He's spoiling for a verbal spar.

Refusing to meet the general's bluster head on, I turn to stare out the shuttle's window at the inky void above the glow of Sunder. Too bad pushing people out into the cold vacuum of space is still illegal.

"The Adamahn are an honorable race, General Alvarez," I say, catching my faint reflection in the glass. My wide face superimposes over Sunder like a dark, omnipresent god who keeps at arms-length

8

from his creation. On the contrary, my mission here is far from arms-length.

"Honorable race? The Adamahn? Ha!" Alvarez throws his head back with dramatic flair. His jet-black hair is typically fashioned in a fresh crew-cut. Shaved high and tight, it's pointy enough to puncture steel with a head-butt. "It's their damn honor that makes them go to war at the drop of a hat!" Alvarez uncrosses his legs like he's ready to spring into action.

The drinking glass in my hand is made of high-tempered Pyrexam, so I can't crush it with my bare hands. Alvarez' simplistic comment gives me the strength to at least try. Sure, I could imagine that it's Alvarez' head, but what would that serve? Could Pyrexam break against the general's big jarhead? I wonder.

Slowly, I turn away from the window back to Alvarez. "The Adamahn's state of constant war has become a drain not only on their resources, but also on their male population. They finally see the futility of this war. Now they're ready to talk. We need to let them."

"Look here, Ambassador, I've been fighting the Adamahn and races like them for some time now and they couldn't give two shits about diplomacy!"

"Why do I get the sense you couldn't give two shits about diplomacy either?" It's men like Alvarez whose mindsets I want to make obsolete.

"I wouldn't say I don't give a shit for the *institution* of diplomacy, Mr. Ambassador," Alvarez says, stretching out his jowls into another grin. "There's a time and a place for it. I leave the scheduling to you *big brains*."

Even seated, Alvarez and his two aides, the unusually stoic Major

Gravely and a female sergeant, puff out their chests in agreement. The three soldiers are ready to show off to the Adamahn all the ribbons and medals they have to impress on this mission: my mission.

"Good thing they don't leave these types of decisions up to you, General," I blurt out sitting high in my chair. "If we had, we would not have known the Adamahn were ready to talk."

Both of my own young aides, Atia Watkins and Cory Murray, squirm at the edge of my peripheral vision. I ignore them, having the confidence to pile on Alvarez. "General, while you were busy shooting spitballs at Prince Falar, I formed back channels with both the Adamahn monarchists *and* the republicans."

Maj. Gravely turns toward me like an old crusty mannequin. His empty expression rests on me for an uncomfortably long time before he decides to speak. "With a man like Tenley Braga in office, the Adamahn will be dealt with swiftly and decisively."

After the statement is delivered with deadpan deliberation, the major faces forward once again as if on a turntable. His commander, Gen. Alvarez, tips his head slightly in approval.

Not to be outdone, I swivel my seat around in a wide arc. "Of all people! Tenley Braga? Really? The man is a joke. Did you see that last debate? Braga didn't understand the tenets of the Tycho Triad Agreement. It's not like that's the only thing keeping the Solar System from erupting into all-out war! Braga had to be prodded for days to speak out against the Lagrange Point separatists and their violence. Have we forgotten how Braga uses separatist rhetoric in his speeches. Not to mention how the Braga brand is stretched so thin. He can't even be taken seriously as a captain of industry anymore, as if he ever was. All of his ventures smack of desperation to stay relevant."

Gravely says nothing in response to my little rant. His pale blue eyes, barely blinking, reveal nothing about what process is going on behind them. His thin lips remain a straight line.

I'm not done and decide to save the best for last. "You know what else, Maj. Gravely? My sources tell me Tenley Braga is not as rich as he would like us to believe."

Once again, the major continues to sit emotionless, staring at me like I'm some lunatic who needs his head examined and dissected.

Gen. Alvarez slaps Gravely on his broad shoulder. "Major, how was it when you met Candidate Braga four days ago at that campaign rally for the troops on Luna?"

The corners of the major's mouth raise by but a hair, the rest of his face remains stolid. "It was great. He is an orator who knows how to speak directly to the people. He understands them. His three sons were impressive, for sure, but his daughter...Oh his daughter was beautiful and smart. It was a life changing experience, if I must say."

Such glowing remarks belie the lack of excitement in Maj. Gravely's voice. It's like he's being paid to say good things about the presidential candidate. If he is, he won't find anyone on *this* shuttle receptive to his political message. This shuttle is full of people on their way to the planet of Sunder, in order to take part in peace talks, in the name of the *incumbent* president of Earth-Gov, George Rebmann.

Gen. Alvarez twists in his seat and gloats about Gravely's story. Not sure why. He wasn't there.

"Braga even gave me a small gift," the major says like it's no big deal.

Gen. Alvarez beams with pride like a father. "Really? I'd like to see it some time."

11

"Don't worry, soon I'll show it." Maj. Gravely makes a series of stiff head and shoulder gestures, like he has a crick in his neck, before continuing. "Braga is a business genius who will bring a firm, stable hand to the chaotic Earth-Gov. Business growth has stagnated on Earth. Braga will change that for the better." Gravely's speech is flat, as if Braga's future is a point of fact. Last I checked, his poll numbers were down 12%.

"Hold on a second!" I say, ready to rain on his parade. "You sound like one of Braga's campaign adverts. Besides, is it not considered bad form for active-duty officers to openly endorse a presidential candidate to civilians? Am I right? Bad form, Major. Simply bad form."

Gen. Alvarez' eyes and bushy brow narrow together into hairy slits as he ignores another jolt of minor turbulence shaking the shuttle. He crosses and uncrosses the tree trunks he calls legs, leaning way forward in his seat as if to really dig into me. I must admit this causes the tiny hairs to prickle at the back of my smooth scalp.

As things heat up, Rebecca French, Deputy Secretary of State, sticks her head out into the aisle. "Gentlemen, let's not have the Adamahn see us in disagreement like this. Okay? We need to show real unity down there. Getting the Adamahn to come all the way to neutral territory, like Sunder, is huge! Sure, the peace deal is one big shit cake, I get it, but everybody has to suck it up and take a slice. So, before we land, let's all get on the same page. Shall we? Sorry Major Gravely, but President Rebmann needs this foreign policy win. Ending the war is why he was elected."

French brushes back her shoulder-length frizzy hair, exposing round chocolate-hued cheeks glowing in the shuttle's harsh fluorescent light. She pauses a beat to let her admonishments sink in before she continues. "By the way, since Tenley Braga thinks these accords are a waste of time and close to treasonous, let's not discuss that divisive son of bitch anymore, shall we?"

Triumphant in shutting both sides down, French shoots me the tiniest of smirks as she sits back in her seat. While I pick my jaw up off the floor, her droopy-eyed deputy assistant, Ken Stubbs, hands her a tablet with documents for her to review. In a hushed tone he says, "-- should stick to business and stay away from politics. Oh wait, Braga's businesses aren't doing so hot either."

They huddle together and share a quick chortle.

Though I'm glad somebody like French is on our side in this conflict, optics do matter. Secretary of State Alexander Cohen should be here heading this meeting, not French. Apparently, he'd prefer to hobnob on the other side of the galaxy with socialites and corporate CEOs than accompany me on a lowly peace accord.

Won't take anything away from French as a replacement. From our past dealings, though few, I find her to be smart as a whip, ten times as shrewd, and fairly attractive. Take the alcohol dispute she mediated between the Belters and the Javagh Corporation. She helped them see there was room for everyone in the market. That was all her. And a few months ago, she persuaded the Slul to come on board as trading partners with Earth-Gov. In exchange for all the Staff Grass they can handle, we received limited teleportation technology. Once we figure out what the hell it is they gave us it'll be revolutionary! All this because of the negotiating skill of one woman, Rebecca French.

While Maj. Gravely continues to stare straight ahead, Gen. Alvarez glares at me like a green uniformed Medusa. Assistant Deputy Secretary Stubbs shrinks way back in his chair, looking for the exits in case a brawl breaks out. Possibly, I went too far. With a modicum of regret, I turn back to my window as another solid wave of turbulence strikes us.

The female sergeant, the other of Alvarez' two aides, pops up and enters the cockpit to finally get some answers, I hope. But she emerges only seconds later after checking in with the pilots. She nudges me. "Ambassador Dylan, Deputy Secretary, aides, please activate your seatbelts. We're on final approach to Sunder's capitol, Ananda."

A quick glance at my watch and I see it has been seven Earth hours since our shuttle departed from the warship, EEF Concorde. While the Concorde was constructed in an expertly utilitarian style proffering the usual dull grays of militarism, Shuttlecraft #1 flies in stark contrast with its polished ivory exterior and desert sands interior. The high-back seats are covered in Ionian leather, providing a comfort unlike anything I've ever experienced. The matching carpet is textured, soft and spotless. The luxurious design aesthetic clearly intended for one purpose: to ferry dignitaries, VIPs and the highest levels of military command around the galaxy to shake hands and kiss babies. In other words, it is designed for comfort and class in the manner of most H-7 Spaceliners. You know the ones only the rich and infamous can afford, somebody like a Tenley Braga.

The button on the armrest activating my seatbelt is tiny and I fumble at it with my fat fingers. When the seatbelt automatically stretches out across my lap, locking itself into place in a latch on the opposite side of my seat, I spy the sergeant's name tag. "Greatly appreciated, Sgt. Jones."

Taken aback, Jones flashes a bright smile from under her black beret, with appreciation that I've addressed her by name. Since she's been attached to this detail, I've noticed how some of the civilian members of this entourage, like Stubbs and French, treat her. To them, she's more like a flight attendant than an important security member of this delegation.

Early on in life, I learned the one word people always love to hear is their name. It means you not only acknowledge them, but you see them as an individual being of value. They're more than some grunt, peon or plebeian. Unfortunately, Jones is one of Gen. Alvarez' lapdogs and susceptible to his jarhead mentality, much like Gravely. She sits with them as they go over security concerns on Sunder.

The shuttle banks left, smooth and easy. Angled at forty-five degrees in relation to the planet, this affords me a spectacular view of the three-band rings encircling Sunder from the starboard window. Light from the system star, Lanx Borealis, passes through the rings' dust, rock and ice, to create an amazing orange-pink glow. In turn, the rings cast a massive shadow on much of the world. Delighted gasps come from the rest of our party when they, too, bear witness to the stunning cosmic display.

Underneath the rings, the shuttle streaks headlong for the equatorial zone. About a thousand kilometers wide, stretching around the entire circumference of Sunder like a belt teeming with life, this range is the warmest and most habitable area of the otherwise deathly cold planet. From this altitude, I view some splashes of green forestation, but they are sparse. Several vast rivers snake their way out of two gargantuan mountain ranges: one northern, one southern. These ranges are all too eager to reach up and scratch us with their icy peaks, so the EEF pilot banks slightly right. That's when we all see it. Curving over the horizon to the north of the equatorial zone, a vast desert stretches out toward forever.

Rebecca French leans toward me across the aisle, one eyebrow raised. "You've been here before, Ambassador. Is that the Great Desert I've heard about?"

Trying my best not to sound like an eggheaded intellectual, I correct her. "It's *one* of The Great Deserts, plural. That's the Northern Desert we're looking at. There's another one in the southern hemisphere just as vast. Both inhumanly cold."

Rebecca French's hazel eyes light up at the concept of learning something new. Her full lips turn up slowly as if invisible strings tug at them, showing perfect teeth. My face flushes with heat as I'm dazzled by her comely features. I swallow hard and angle my gaze to the floor of the cabin.

The shuttle's intercom comes to my rescue.

"If you look out your windows," drones the pilot, a Captain Fukuwara. "You can see Sunder's massive capitol city, Ananda at Eleven and one o'clock."

"Eleven and one o'clock? I don't get it." My aide, Cory Murray, looks from left to right scratching his temple. Blond-haired, tall and thick-necked, he is great at breaking down governmental policy, but possessing day-to-day common sense, not so much.

Before I can set the young man straight, my other aide, Atia Watkins, takes up the mantle. "Kinda straight ahead, Cory! Eleven and one!" Atia makes the hands of a clock with her petite arms and rolls her big brown eyes. "And if you're wondering, twelve o'clock is the cockpit!"

Cory, tongue-tied, shrugs his sloped shoulders and resumes staring out of his window.

Through some more turbulence, the pilot maneuvers the shuttle above a deep, pink-tinted valley gouged out between two mountain ranges. On the horizon, the massive phosphorescent dome of the city of Ananda is open for our arrival. The gleam of great silver and white spires show off their architectural genius as they stretch upward to greet the shuttle streaking overhead.

"Ananda, what a wonderful name!" Deputy Secretary French declares to no one in particular. "The city is simply stunning!"

"It sure is." I chime in unable to help myself. "Originally, Ananda was known as the City of Memory by the ancient Sunderians because of their history of establishing so many famous libraries. Now it's most famous for The Archive Tower: hi-tech home of countless interplanetary archives, corporate data, government intelligence and sensitive information for billions of beings. All of it stored throughout a complex composed of several connected data centers."

Rebecca French stares at me, mouth agape. "I was told you're familiar with the Tower, but no one told me you were an expert!" She pauses as if waiting for me to regale her with tales of adventure instead of the boring meetings I attended during past state visits.

"I'm familiar," I tell her, as I try to recall something interesting from that time. "Oh, the last time I visited, which was two years ago, I was on a diplomatic tour to assure the Nefertarians it was safe to store their data here. They're so mistrusting."

"So, I've heard." French stifles a girlish giggle. "I can't wait for our visit there tomorrow. Your knowledge of Sunder and the Archive Tower is pretty impressive, Ambassador Dylan!"

I'd hazard a guess French is accustomed to President Rebmann's ambassadorial appointments being old money cronies like her Boss,

Alexander Cohen, not someone trained in political science and history like myself. This is the perfect opportunity to show her ambassadors can be appointed for their expertise in a thing or two and not because someone is owed a favor for their political donations. Although, the President *does* owe me a few favors.

"You used to be a teacher, right?" French tilts her head slightly showing how her copper-toned chin could be both soft and strong at the same time.

"University professor to be exact." I fold my hands to keep from fidgeting. "For seven years I was in academia. Even some bank robbers don't get sentenced for that length of time."

There goes my *gift* — to say things out loud I hadn't intended. My gut sinks with dread.

Rebecca looks confused at first before she lets out a bizarre laugh from deep within her flat stomach. To see someone so attractive with such an odd cachinnate, can be a bit jarring.

"Why, you're hilarious, Ambassador!" Rebecca throws her curly hair back and crosses her dancer-sculpted legs. Pretending to laugh it off, I return my gaze back to Ananda.

"Thank God Ananda's located in the equatorial zone! Eh, Ambassador?" Atia Watkins saves me from my bashfulness.

"God had nothing to do with it."

"And why's that, sir?" Atia cocks her head letting thin braids rest on her shoulder.

"It was planned for Ananda to be built along the equator, so Sunder's records could have the best chance at survival."

"Survival?" Atia's small face scrunches up.

"You see, most of the planet is in the process of being claimed by

18

The Great Deserts. About a thousand years ago, Sunderian scientists discovered the planet's core is cooling."

"Cooling?" Rebecca French leans back into the conversation. "Why is that?"

"No one can truly ascertain the cause. One theory, and there are many, is it has to do with the Great Cataclysm which occurred during what Sunderians call, The Ancient Era."

"What happened during *The Great Cataclysm*?" Rebecca clasps her hands together, digging in for a good story.

Always happy to recount some good history, I focus on the radiance in Rebecca's eyes. "According to the records, there were planet-wide quakes devastating much of the world. And as the world recovered, their scientists noticed years later the deserts which had formed over geologic time in their prehistoric past, were now spreading and merging. This is how the Great Northern and Southern Deserts came to be. Further study of the planet's core in those areas found it cooling. Perfect for storing data. Eventually, the core cooling will erode the electromagnetic field surrounding Sunder, leaving it defenseless against the solar radiation of Lanx Borealis. But that won't be for millions of years."

"That's so sad," Rebecca sighs, rapt with full attention.

I continue. "Elsewhere on Sunder, life can only exist within the many domes which provide heat, proper atmospheric pressure, and protection from the increased radiation out in the desert."

"Wow, that's amazing, Ambassador! Isn't it Deputy Secretary French?" Atia says like the perfect wing-woman I know she is.

Meanwhile, my other aide, Cory Murray, continues to sit dumbfounded at the sight of the city, his face pressed against his window like a kid outside a toy store. His big teeth almost get knocked out when another wave of turbulence jostles us with more force than before. Everyone becomes wide-eyed, searching each other's expressions for answers. I grip my armrests like a constrictor clutching its latest meal. Only General Alvarez and the ever-stoic Major Gravely are unfazed. As the shuttle vibrates up and down and side to side, these two men are as stiff as the dead.

Rebecca wheels around to Sgt. Jones. "Maybe the pilot should tell us something."

Sgt. Jones, sporting a not-so-bad poker face, stares at the deputy secretary with her big blue eyes. After a long moment, she looks at her commander for the go ahead. Gen. Alvarez gives her a stern nod and Jones is up again, stumbling toward the cockpit, fighting against the rocking of the cabin. In one motion, Sgt. Jones slides past the threshold and closes the door behind her. But before she does, a flurry of activity is exposed inside among the pilots. One battles against the controls while barking indistinct orders to his co-pilot. He, in turn, slaps at buttons and switches with the fury of a frightened tiger.

Feeling for my seatbelt, I make sure it's secure. The shuttle picks up speed, jostling, dipping, then ascending at odd angles. After an eternity of this, Sgt. Jones emerges agitated. She makes a beeline to her seat, strapping in tight, and adjusts the beret on her blond-bunned head.

"Well?" Rebecca French throws up her hands. For a brief moment, Sgt. Jones gives the Deputy Secretary an empty stare before turning to her commander as if wondering if she should answer to a civilian.

For the benefit of the deputy secretary, Gen. Alvarez gives his lapdog permission to speak. "What's the situation, Jones?"

Shaken, Sgt. Jones continues to check her seatbelt. "The pilot said we're not experiencing turbulence, sir!"

"Not experiencing turbulence?" Rebecca says, her voice scratches the ceiling of the cabin.

"None of it is turbulence," Sgt. Jones rushes. "The pilot said it's not engine trouble either, sir!"

"What the hell else is it?" Gen. Alvarez' gaze bounces back and forth between Jones and the cockpit door. "Tractor beam? EMP attack?"

Jones talks directly to her commander and no one else. "Capt. Fukuwara said it's the shuttle's computer. There's something wrong with the software for the controls, sir!"

"I see." Alvarez is as calm as a pond-scum filled lake.

The co-pilot, a Lt. Lincoln, comes on the intercom. "Ladies and gentlemen, our destination was to be the Dullen Interplanetary Spaceport. But due to a catastrophic failure of the software system of this shuttlecraft, we will have to make an emergency landing one and a half clicks away. I have notified space traffic control and they will prepare for our arrival. I'm attempting to reboot the shuttle's control computer as Capt. Fukuwara flies manually. At this time, I ask that you assume the crash position. Capt. Fukuwara is one of the best there is and he will do his best to get us down safely. In the meantime, please feel free to pray and or commune with the deity of your choice. Thank you."

Great, just when I'd become a firm agnostic.

Quickly, I force my torso to mash against my knees, in an attempt to ride out the flight. Alvarez and Gravely calmly lean over and do the same. The shuttle banks hard left and my stomach sinks. Without warning, we drop into a steep accelerated descent. The blare of emergency alarms barrels through me with a deafening haze, slowing down time. I forget to breathe but sneak a peek outside the shuttle. Skyscrapers, airbuses, and air cars merge into a blur as we scream past them. The cabin points down at a steep angle. Anything not tacked down in the back of the shuttle, like cups, snacks, stationery, gets dumped forward. For a fleeting moment, perhaps enhanced by fear and adrenaline, anything which isn't nailed down hangs suspended in the pressurized air as gravity ceases in this parabolic drop. A large packet of coffee, floating a few centimeters from my nose with the grace of a seasoned aerialist, spews its nutty aroma. Another lurch of the shuttle jerks me back into real-time and the craft out of the parabola. Tablets, computers, and briefcases go flying now that gravity re-establishes itself. The entire delegation is showered with plastic cups, plates, utensils, and trash from the galley. A hale of glasses, liquor bottles and beer cans, is sent crashing to the front of the cabin, shattering against the cockpit door. A bottle of Aviatrix '23 narrowly misses my head. I'm pelted hard in my calf by a can of disgusting squirtberry juice. Luggage, leather bags, and diplomatic gifts tumble out of the overhead bins in a hard rain. My briefcase misses my head by centimeters. Out of the side of my eye, I witness Rebecca's aide, Ken Stubbs, take a painful shot to his shoulder from a heavy suitcase. The case continues forward, clipping Gen. Alvarez' outstretched leg, finally coming to rest at the front of the cabin. Along with the debris, screams, sobs, and shrieks bounce off the walls. Our cries are drowned out by the shrill squeal of upper atmosphere rushing past our craft. Any moment, the ground will come up and meet us, ending it all before my mission is to begin. It's not fair.

The deafening cry of our craft's nosedive is soon replaced by a new sound, that of a deep, guttural groan. It's as if the shuttle is going through birth pangs when the metal hull protests against the external stresses imposed upon it.

From underneath, pressure pushes up against me. Is the shuttle's nose tipping upward? First, it's slight, then it increases ever so gradually. I sneak another peek out my window. Degree by degree, the craft is leveling off! I can't believe the pilot has regained control!

But I can tell we are still losing altitude. If I wasn't belted in, my seat would drop out from underneath me. The shuttle continues to shake violently, threatening to rattle the craft apart. Strong vibrations surge through the soles of my shoes, up my spine. The thunderous rumble of the retro-jets come online, slowing our descent. God, is it enough? Panicked, I glance out my window only to see us fall below the top of the city's famous skyline. A second later the shuttle slams with one jarring belly flop, jerking us all upright out of our crash positions. We bounce hard like a metal ball and everything airborne inside the cabin comes crashing down again. My broad shoulders and thick football player's neck have trouble keeping my big head still, as I'm whiplashed fiercely in my seat. The seatbelt is stretched to its limits. The craft skids violently, not wanting to stop. Dirt kicks up past the windows. A grinding screech rips into my eardrums. Shredded metal spits up sparks that shower up the craft's sides and into view. After seconds, which feel like minutes, the shuttle finally comes to a rest.

Light smoke seeps into the back of the shuttle and pricks at the back of my nose and throat. Thankfully, there is no fire...yet. Nothing on me is fractured or cut, but I do hurt from the seat-belt's contact points. Moans and cries fill the air. I crane my neck around to see who is hurt. Scanning the trashed cabin, I can't discern who it's coming from.

"Is anyone injured?" I call out, prompting the moans to grow louder.

With a click of the quick release seatbelt, I'm up and in the direction of the moans. It is my aide, Cory. He is in serious pain. His right arm has a bend which should not be there. "Hold on, Cory. Try not to move. Emergency services should be on their way."

"I can't believe this is happening!" Cory groans. His eyes are squeezed tight as he gingerly holds his damaged arm with his other. Quickly, I remove my tie and make a sling.

Ken Stubbs pops out of his restraints and quickly attends to Rebecca French. "You okay?"

She unfastens her seatbelt and waves him off. "I'll live." She shoots me a quick smile and brushes off debris.

"Atia, how are you doing?" She's fumbling with her seatbelt, so I step through the debris littering the aisle to assist her.

"I...think I'm...good," she says between sobs, letting me unfasten her.

Gen. Alvarez, Maj. Gravely and Sgt. Jones are already out of their seats assessing the damage. Alvarez points. "Gravely, check the cockpit. Make sure the pilots are okay. Jones, get everyone off this heap!"

Stone-faced, Gravely trudges to the cockpit and forces the door with little effort. Capt. Fukuwara staggers out helping his physically distressed co-pilot. Lt. Lincoln holds his left hand away from his body. It's covered in the oddest-looking burns: black dots that pulsate.

Sgt. Jones, meanwhile, shoves open the hatch allowing midday light to beam inside the cabin. She directs Rebecca French to leave who says she won't until her assistant leaves first. You don't have to tell Stubbs twice. He wastes little time jumping out of the hatch and onto the ground kicking up grass and dirt. Then and only then does the Deputy Secretary exit. While I make sure Atia is ahead of me, Sgt. Jones jumps out to the ground to help my aide exit. Quickly, I hand off Cory. "Careful, Sgt. Jones, his arm is broken."

"I got him, Mr. Ambassador."

I refuse to exit the wreck just yet. There is something about the co-pilot, Lt. Lincoln. Something about his hand. Something familiar.

"Are you okay, Airman?" I ask, but he only moans and is close to passing out. Right before my eyes, his hand has become this grotesque swollen appendage covered in black pulsating spots.

Capt. Fukuwara shakes his head while he helps the co-pilot to the hatch, incredulous about our turn of events. "The helm-computer went haywire! Lincoln tried to fix it and he gets attacked! I did all I could to get us down in one piece! You have to believe me!"

Lincoln attacked? What is Fukuwara talking about? Attacked by who?

Stepping over debris to get to the cockpit, I stick my head in. The helm-computer is in the center. On top of it and all around it are little black spots — spots that pulsate and move in and out of the computer. "Holy shit! Those are — "

Before I can finish the thought, my neck and shoulder are suddenly caught in a vice-like grip. Maj. Gravely stares at me like I am a nuisance to be removed, not a passenger who might need aid. He does not speak. He squeezes tight, using the pain to direct me away from the cockpit like some cold mama tiger carrying her wayward cub from mischief. The man practically gives me the bum's rush out the hatch.

"Come, Ambassador. Evacuate." Gen. Alvarez shows little distress about the predicament we are in. "This shuttle can explode at any minute."

Gravely and Alvarez follow me off the shuttle. Alvarez shoos us further away. "Move as far away as possible, people! No telling what kind of damage has been done to the fuel lines!"

Obeying his orders for now, our delegation stumbles and limps away from the wreck. After about fifty meters most of us flop down on the torn-up lawn, broken and exhausted. Fear-induced adrenaline already starts to wear off in me, leaving me sore all over. We've settled in the middle of what is a wide clearing in a massive park on the edge of the city. The shuttle dug a trench into the greenery about half a klick long! Acrid smoke from the wreckage stings my lungs and throat, even at this distance. Amongst our rabble, I look for the two pilots. When I find them, I see the black spots burrowing into the arm of the now unconscious Lt. Lincoln.

"I don't know what's happening to him." Our pilot, Fukuwara says. His smoke-stung eyes search me for answers.

Although I am still processing the event of my near-death, I still have the wherewithal to know exactly what I'm looking at. So, I give it to him straight. "You should stand away from him, Captain. Far away. That goes for everyone else!"

Now everyone's attention shifts to me. "Your man, Lincoln, has been infected with nanites," I explain. Gasps sound off along with denials. I continue. "They were probably intended for the shuttle's computer systems. Someone wants us all dead!"

Chapter Two

"Nanites?" Atia asks. She's sitting on the grass wiping away more tears. "You mean those microscopic machine things that repair stuff?" Through red eyes she tries to help Sgt. Jones tend to a prone Cory and his broken arm.

"In a nutshell, yes," I say. "Somehow they were introduced into the shuttle's helm computer system."

Ken Stubbs points at the wrecked shuttle. "So, this was no accident?"

"Like I said. It's sabotage, yes."

"By whom?" Rebecca French demands, angrier than scared. I have to admit I am too.

Gen. Alvarez spins around like a tiger who's had its tail yanked. "Who do you think, Deputy Secretary? It was those Adamahn sons of bitches!"

"How, General?" Rebecca snaps back. "We haven't had direct contact with the Adamahn yet! There were no spies on the Concorde and security swept for unauthorized surveillance!" Rebecca waves her arms, incredulous the Adamahn could be capable of such subterfuge. She turns to me seeking answers. "How?"

I try to sound confident. "It doesn't make sense for the Adamahn. This isn't their way."

"Not their way?" Gen. Alvarez paces in anger. "They are a bunch of back-stabbing, sneak-thieving murderers!"

"Not the tribes I've been dealing with!" Again, I am losing my patience with this man. "The Adamahn want these accords to work out as much as we do!"

The general stops pacing and stands before me, one side of his mouth curled up. "Well, there must be a tribe you don't know about, smart guy! One that doesn't like our handholding and song-singing!"

Alvarez' theory does not make sense for the one reason only I knew. "Listen, General. There is no way the Adamahn could have access to the nanites."

The general puffs out his chest. "Big deal! Someone could have given or sold that junk to them."

"That's true, Ambassador." Rebecca says, as if grasping for any reason to give to Earth-Gov.

I point at Lt. Lincoln's hand. "Not *these* nanites."

Rebecca walks right up to me, uncomfortably close, her eyes soft but demanding. "What's so special about these nanites?"

"Well...Based on their characteristic movement and how they were deployed, these nanites are registered trademarked as *Dagerites*."

"Dagerites?" Rebecca echoes.

"They were named after a forgotten tech specialist at a tiny tech firm called Rosenfeld Labs. Dagerites are used primarily as a subterfuge weapon. When introduced into an enemy computer system they either rewrite the software with predetermined programming or they simply knock that system off-line."

Behind Rebecca's glassy, hazel eyes, questions begin to form. "Ok, that explains the shuttle's computer, but what's going on with our co-pilot's hand?"

I walk over to Lt. Lincoln, careful not to get too close. Drenched in sweat, his breathing is shallow and ragged, his hand now black with Dagerites. "Like I said, he's been infected."

Using a stick, I push back the sleeve to his flight jacket and notice his forearm muscles twitching in a wave of spasms. I continue with my explanation. "Dagerites infect both inorganic *and* organic systems. That discovery was unfortunately made by Mr. Dager himself. He accidentally infected himself, causing his higher-mind functions to be wiped clean."

Everyone shifts their focus to Lt. Lincoln. Atia, Cory and Fukuwara's faces turn ashen, Rebecca and Stubbs look elsewhere as if not wanting to show their discomfort, while Alvarez and Jones recoil away. Only Maj. Gravely stands listening; his face etched into a nondescript countenance.

"How long does he have?" Capt. Fukuwara asks. "You know, before he's *wiped clean*."

"I'm not sure." I reply, tugging at a string to one of my memories. "The few witnesses there were mentioned under an hour, maybe thirty minutes, maybe less."

Lines form along Fukuwara's forehead. "What about survivors?"

My initial reaction is to blurt out 'what survivors?' but I can see these pilots are close. Instead, I shake my head. The lines on Fukuwara's forehead deepen.

Ken Stubbs gets into my face. "If Rosenfeld Labs no longer exists, why the hell are these Dagerites still around? Look how dangerous they are!"

Overwhelmed, I take two steps back from Stubbs before continuing. "Some... saw the dangers and wanted them shut down, while others... saw the military applications. Of course, the latter won out." I glance over at a smug Gen. Alvarez. With an eyebrow cocked, he visibly gives the idea a thought.

"How do you know so much about these Dagerites, Ambassador?" Rebecca asks, hands on her hips like a mother wondering why her child missed curfew.

All eyes are now on me as the delegation becomes rapt listeners. "Well... um, five years ago, back when I was a senator and chairman of the Earth-Gov Senate Intelligence Committee, a Nebvolian terrorist cell held six hostages on the moon, Vorle. Earth-Gov approved an operation to rescue them and decided this was a good opportunity to see the Dagerites in action."

Cory, now sitting up, holds his arm in my makeshift sling and grits his teeth. "Nebvolian terrorists? Please tell me those bastards got taken out good and hard."

I take a deliberate step toward the upright Cory. "Oh, the Dagerites were effective, alright. Carried by a liquid solution, they were introduced into the air vents of the terrorists' stronghold in the form of an aerosol mist. The buggers worked as advertised. The terrorists were immediately infected and summarily mind-wiped — and so were the hostages."

Everyone's eyes widen. A gasp escapes from Atia.

Capt. Fukuwara, kneeling next to his co-pilot, backs away a few centimeters. "Oh God, is that going to happen to Lincoln?" Dark eyes stare at the infected hand as it slowly returns to its normal flesh-tone. But the eerie Dagerites continue to crawl back and forth underneath the skin, causing it to distend and bubble. They burrow deeper into his flesh, entering his bloodstream.

"I don't know if that's going to happen, Captain," I say watching the Dagerites work their way up Lincoln's arm. "What I do know is we need to get him medical assistance fast."

Sgt. Jones checks her comm. "Emergency services say they're ten minutes out."

Rebecca implores me to finish my tale with a twirl of her hand. "Ambassador, what happened with the Dagerites after Vorle?"

"There was a rushed emergency session with the Intelligence Committee. We came together to decide what to do about the Dagerites. Unanimously, the Committee voted to ban them."

Gen. Alvarez resumes his pacing, grumbling at Maj. Gravely. "If I was in charge of that op, it wouldn't have gone sideways like that."

Maj. Gravely does not respond.

Ego at a time like this gets a swift eye roll from me. "Really, General? You would've been mind-wiped too." Might not have been a bad thing, now that I think about it.

"As I was saying. With our decision to ban the Dagerites, Rosenfeld Labs' stock fell through the floor. They had a fire sale. Divisions of the company were sliced off like a Christmas ham and gobbled up by several corporations. The Intelligence Committee monitored the sale of each division."

"And who, pray-tell, bought the nanotech division?" Rebecca asks.

"Rosenfeld's nanotechnology division was bought by Braga Works. I suggested them since they barely make any innovation in that sector. The price tag was raised ridiculously high to prevent a bidding war. Two months later, the sale was approved with my deciding vote."

At the mention of the purchasing company's name, Maj. Gravely, face blank, turns his broad body toward me in a rigid sweep. He cocks his square head to listen but remains silent. Maybe he's too surprised to find his hero's company involved in such a risky venture.

Red rage ignites within Rebecca's eyes. "Braga Works? Tenley Braga was the buyer? That son of a bitch!"

Atia, her eyes still red and puffy, finally stops crying. But her voice quivers with distress. "Wait! *The* Tenley Braga? Billionaire industrialist Braga? Presidential candidate Braga?!"

Cory winces from pain as he chimes in. "Ha! Ha! I get Braga wanting to kill you, Deputy Secretary; President Rebmann being your boss and all, but why kill the rest of us?"

"C'mon, Cory!" Atia scolds my policy wonk. "You joke too much!"

"Sorry, jeez." Cory puts on a hang-dog pout.

"You might be on to something though." Atia continues. "Someone in Braga Works must have found out about the Dagerites."

"Pretty sure it's not Tenley Braga." Cory says. "He's more of an angel investor-type than a hands-on kind of owner. He buys, re-brands, and flips so many companies and products, I'm sure he has no clue what he's getting half the time. The guy was still hawking Braga Burgers on the vids, in the days just before he announced his candidacy! He's ridiculous! A complete clown! They're not bad, you know. The burgers I mean."

Rebecca rolls her eyes before turning to me. "Ambassador, are you sure only Braga Works could have access to the Dagerites? No other company?"

My mind's eye plays back the events of the Senate committee hearing. The dim chamber in the Capitol building, closed to the public and press. The pictures of the victims on Vorle and their hospitalizations. The magnified images of the Dagerites, black beetle-like machines floating in a blood sample, passed around between senators. The fat stacks of paperwork listing the companies now owning each partition of Rosenfeld Labs down to the stationery. Was there something we missed?

"Anything is possible." My mind races through the possibilities. "Our committee's investigation was pretty damn thorough. We ordered, by decree, the destruction of any and all prototypes, product, and research, or so I believed. Any other information about the Dagerites was buried deep on Earth and here on Sunder. Anyone associated with Braga Works couldn't have known! They shouldn't have known, unless they did some serious digging and discovered it by accident."

"Well Ambassador, someone knows." Rebecca's harsh tone sucks the air out of me. She spins away to her assistant, Ken Stubbs. Does she believe what I already feel; *my* intelligence committee is to blame for this? That we didn't do our due diligence? That maybe there was a leak?

She rages with Stubbs. "I cannot wait to give this to the media. I'll let *them* burn Tenley Braga's ass at the stake."

"You can bet that snake oil salesman doesn't have a clue about the little monsters his company purchased," Stubbs adds.

"Doesn't matter." Rebecca tosses off the assumption for what I know to be the bigger prize she could gift to her boss. "Once the press gets a hold of this scandal, his presidential bid will be over!"

"I'll hit up my contacts at GNN, The Times and *The Spencer Report,*" Stubbs declares punching buttons on his mobile.

"Don't forget *The Dahlgren Desk!*" Rebecca points out with a well-manicured finger. "I can't wait to see how they'll spin this in his favor. But we've got Spencer in *our* pocket so that will cancel out Dahlgren."

"On it! The headlines will read, 'Tenley Braga, unwitting owner of deadly nanotech! Unwitting as President?'" Stubbs traces imaginary double headlines in mid-air.

Rebecca and Stubbs burst into uncontrolled laughter. For the two of them, it's already Election Night in this park clearing and the results are in. Their victory celebration has already begun with the prospect of revealing to the entire solar system that a company owned by presidential rival, Tenley Braga, has a connection to some miniature machines with deadly directives.

But the elation brought on by their *win* is short-lived as Ken Stubbs' eyes grow wide and blink rapidly. His mouth falls open as he raises his hand as if in a defensive posture.

"Rebecca, look out!" Ken yells, pushing Rebecca to the ground. There is a loud crack from behind me on my left and Ken goes flying backward at least five meters. He lands hard clutching his stomach and groaning aloud. On the front of his light-gray business suit, a red stain spreads out from beneath his hands.

Chapter Three

Behind me, holding a smoking service pistol pointed in the direction of Ken Stubbs and Rebecca French, stands Maj. Jaylend Gravely. His expression, which barely changed this entire trip, resembles etchings in a block of cold granite. Atia screams in high-pitched terror. Cory pops up and snatches the young woman to her feet with his good arm, ignoring the pain in the other. Sgt. Jones ushers both away from the fray and shields them with her body. Along the way, she fumbles for her own service weapon. Gen. Alvarez springs into action, grabbing Maj. Gravely in a bear hug from behind. "Stand down, soldier! Stand down!"

The two men grapple and struggle with all their might. Impressive for his age, Alvarez tries to pick Gravely up off his feet. But Gravely shakes free of his commander like a greased pig. Deploying strength beyond what's typically found in EEF soldiers, the major grabs the general and tosses him to the ground with ease. Gravely swings his large frame back around toward the rest of us. Small, dark eyes scan the grass, settling on a stunned Rebecca as she sits upright in the clearing. Stiff as an iron rod, Gravely slowly raises his service weapon.

Not content to be a mere shocked spectator, I yank the deputy secretary to her feet and make for the tree line. The others follow my lead. Gravely fires two more shots. Bullets whiz past my ear, blowing off a thick yellow-green branch from a tree to my left. We slide behind thick bushes and lay flat. Alvarez scrambles to his feet, tucks in his shoulder and uses his solid frame to blindside Gravely like a lead blocker in football. Gravely goes down hard, rolling over several times, kicking up a cloud of dirt, but never loses his service weapon. This buys all those who can stand time to make it to the trees. Gen. Alvarez shakes his head in dismay, wondering what's Maj. Gravely's problem.

As Alvarez jogs toward the woods, his mad subordinate, awkwardly and methodically, sits upright. The general ducks behind the cover of brush some ten meters away from me. He may not be a young man, but Gen. Alvarez manages to shock me at how much speed, strength, and fight he has in him.

Behind the tree line, dense purple and neon green brush native to Sunder shields us. I lie flat on the mossy, forest ground, keeping quiet. In heaving drags, I cough up dirt I managed to inhale during our mad scramble for cover. Rebecca's hand is cold and clammy as I still grip it tight. Although she doesn't seem to mind or notice, slowly, I release it.

"Oh my God!" Rebecca lifts her head to peek into the clearing. "Why is he doing this? Why?"

I push her head back down roughly. "Sh-sh. He can't see all of us."

Fifteen meters to my left, Capt. Fukuwara is prone and breathing hard, forced to abandon his unconscious co-pilot. About thirty meters to my right, though I can't see her, Atia screams her head off in abject panic. Maj. Gravely shoots once in the direction of my assistant. I can only pray he's missed his target.

Gen. Alvarez grimaces as if Atia's continued screams pierce his eardrums. "Shut her up for God's sake!"

A scuffle arises and Atia's screams become muffled into whimpers. I can only assume it must be Cory or Sgt. Jones gagging the poor girl.

"Gravely, what the hell are you doing?" Gen. Alvarez yells without raising from his stomach.

Gravely answers with a single report from his service weapon. The shot kicks up dirt to the left of Gen. Alvarez. "Son of a bitch," he mutters then shuffles backward and to his right.

From the area of Atia's whimpering, a muzzle flash lights up part of the brush accompanied by a loud bang. Maj. Gravely stumbles backward several steps, his left arm dangles from a gunshot wound to the shoulder. Sgt. Jones vaults out from behind the brush, scrambles behind a large tree, and points her service pistol at the major with two hands, her arms fully extended.

"Major! What are you doing? Drop your weapon!" Sgt. Jones pleads. "It's me, Rhoda! I don't want to hurt you!"

Wavering back and forth, Gravely remains silent. He glares at the tree Jones uses for cover before he unleashes two more shots that rip away the light brown tree bark.

"Don't make me do this, Jaylend!" Jones cocks her head to the left side for the eye she uses to aim.

"Jaylend Gravely is doing his duty." The major intones like a bad actor in one of those YouStar video shows. He makes stiff motions with his body as he attempts to get an angle on Jones.

Since the start of this mission, Gravely spoke few words. When he did speak, it was with a voice resonating in a deep monotone. It's different now. Still deep, but tonally lighter, as if another voice is layered on top of it.

"Young Maj. Gravely is doing his duty." The major repeats, covering his wounded shoulder with his gun hand.

"What does he mean?" Rebecca whispers to me, her pixie face

covered in Sunderian dirt. "Why is he referring to himself like that?"

A spark of revelation burns in my mind. "I learned about this during the committee hearings. Remember how I said the Dagerites can overwrite software? They can overwrite the brain's higher functions as well, not just wipe them clean."

"Overwrite the brain?" Rebecca's face falls. "Wait! Gravely's infected? You mean those things can change a person's thoughts to whatever *someone else* wants?"

Lying flat on my stomach, amidst the colorful flora of a beautiful Sunderian park, with death lurking mere meters away, my response to Rebecca is even more sobering. "The real threat of the Dagerites — mind-control."

Rebecca inches her head up to peek through the brush again at who used to be Maj. Gravely. "My God. A zombie army at one's command."

Like an after-hours drunk spoiling for a fight, Gravely saunters from side to side. His left arm hangs limp. His good arm waves his service pistol in wide arcs, hoping for more of us to show ourselves.

I rise on my elbows. "Hey, if you're not Gravely, who the hell are you?"

Gravely smiles, pointing the pistol in the general direction of my voice. He doesn't fire, instead preferring to play games with his prey. "I'm Maj. Gravely and Maj. Gravely does his duty!"

I give Capt. Fukuwara an examining look. "Where's your service weapon?"

The captain frowns. "It's still on the shuttle."

I roll my eyes and shift my gaze to Gravely. "Whoever you are, what do you want?"

"I want a great many things, Ambassador." Gravely shakes his pistol with every word. "I want power, control. You know, the usual! But right now, I'll settle for you and your friends dead."

38

He squeezes off a shot, splitting the brush directly over my head, Green and violet vegetation splatter in every direction, forcing me back onto my belly.

"What the hell, man? Stop it! Major, don't make me do this!" Sgt. Jones yells. She has not come to the same conclusions Rebecca, and I have. With desperation belying her strong voice, she once again tries to reach the Gravely who no longer resides within.

Gravely unleashes a stilted laugh. "There is nothing you can do, Sergeant! But Maj. Gravely, he does his duty."

"This is insane," Rebecca whispers.

Raising up on my elbows again, I regain my view of Gravely. Awkwardly, he cranes his neck to see if anyone will foolishly pop their head up. He turns back toward my direction. "Come out everyone! Why prolong the inevitable?"

Rebecca has had enough; her ire finally bubbles over. "You bastard! Screw you! Why do you want us dead?"

"I have my reasons, Deputy Secretary French!" Gravely walks toward the tree line grinning, weapon at the ready.

"Your *reasons*?" Rebecca yells. "Or maybe it's more like your *orders*! Who's really running your black op?"

Gravely stops in his tracks. "Why couldn't you just let the shuttle crash and burn in one big, beautiful conflagration of assumed Adamahn sabotage! Now...things are going to get...messy."

Gravely shakes his head like he is truly sorry he has to murder us. He can shove his false pity and not do me any favors.

"Enough talk!" Gen. Alvarez bellows. "Sgt. Jones, take that fool down now! That's an order!"

"Sir, yes, sir!" Sgt. Jones responds to her superior with a great deal of pleasure in her voice. She slips out from behind the tree cover. Her automatic pistol spits three times, hitting the possessed Gravely center mass. He falls back as air escapes him aloud like a vacuum sealed room has suddenly been opened. Soon, the only sound is the rustling of leaves by a stray breeze.

"Is he dead?" Rebecca looks at me dazed, breathing heavily. "Please tell me he's dead, Dylan."

"I'm not sure." I stick my head out from the colorful brush.

Gravely lay on his back, motionless. His large arms stretch out like the letter 'Y.' His service weapon lies a few meters away from him. His legs are crossed at the ankles like he's relaxed at a picnic, daydreaming to soft music. From my periphery, Sgt. Jones emerges, cautious as a cat. Handgun still at the ready, each step is measured and deliberate. Once she reaches Gravely, she kicks his foot twice. No response.

"He's down!" Sgt. Jones announces, subdued.

I look to Rebecca. "Gravely or whoever the hell...he's dead."

Cory springs out from the bushes pumping the fist of his good arm. "Yeah, that's what I'm talking about, Jonesie!"

The sergeant sticks out her chin and nods thanks.

Rebecca pushes herself up on her knees and spies through the brush. She places a hand over her heart, satisfied our would-be assassin is dead. Her body jerks as if a loud noise has gone off inside only her head, causing her to glance to the left of Gravely's corpse. "My God, Ken!"

The Deputy Secretary is on her feet and bursts from the bushes with the ferocity of a mama bear. I follow.

"Ken, are you alright?" She pleads. "Ken, talk to me! Are you okay?"

Ken Stubbs rolls gingerly onto his side and groans. "No, I'm not okay! It hurts pretty bad! Tried to play dead!"

Rebecca gets a good look at the wound. "He needs a medic! Where's the damn emergency services? They should be here by now!"

Sgt. Jones checks the comm on her wrist. "They're real close."

40

"Step aside, Deputy Secretary!" Gen. Alvarez marches forward. "I still have my field dressing skills."

The general bends down and rolls Ken Stubbs onto his back. "Let me take a look, Stubbs." He takes off his jacket and tears off the sleeve to his shirt. With it, he presses hard against Stubbs' abdomen.

"If I can slow the bleeding, you might have a chance."

Chapter Four

In the distance, the rhythmic thumping of a medi-thopter's rotor blades keeps time with my heart. It is the prelude to the siren song of six Sunderian fire thopters soaring over the treetops into the clearing. Maybe I'm concussed, but the grateful sight hypnotizes me as their rotors power gale-force winds into the alien glade, rocking trees sideways and kicking up dirt and loose vegetation. When they land, a small army of emergency services personnel spills out in a blur of activity. A fire team, covered in heavy metallic clothing and masks, examines the smoldering wreck of the shuttle while teams of green-skinned Sunderian paramedics immediately attend to Ken Stubbs. A sole paramedic pays close attention to Cory's arm, now in a flex splint, ushering my policy wonk onto a waiting thopter. Behind them, on a levitating med-evac gurney, Ken Stubbs is loaded onto the same thopter. Still conscious, Stubbs reminds Rebecca about the finer points of Adamahn conversational strategy with surprising coherence. Once he is safely tucked into the thopter, Rebecca turns on her heels kicking up a mini dust devil. She barks orders to the paramedics about how her assistant must be treated because of her importance to EarthGov and his importance to her. The excitement has died down, but the adrenaline remains in my bloodstream, causing my mind to slide into a fugue state. I barely register the quick vertical rise of the medical thopter before it zooms off over the treetops for a hospital somewhere in the city center of Ananda.

Seated on the grass, Atia pulls her knees to her chest. She tries to fight the involuntary urge to rock back and forth, so a paramedic offers her a sedative. As if snapping out of a trance, she stops to badger the paramedic about what's in it. Not far from them, Gen. Alvarez, like a wound care maestro, points to all the cuts and bruises covering his arms and hands. He directs the paramedics, who attend to him, where to spray the synth-skin bandages. Sgt. Jones, meanwhile, tries to wave off the paramedic who attempts to lend her aid. Her stiff-arm technique and dramatic scowl are no match for the dedication of the paramedic, who dutifully sprays her forehead and legs with synth-skin.

While a paramedic examines the scratches I received from both the crash and the crawl through the brush, I snap to when a medical team approaches Lt. Lincoln. Once I alert them about his infection, the team goes into quarantine protocols. Each paramedic taps a button on their ID badges. Bio-hazard hoods and visors sprout out from their uniforms, covering the paramedics' heads and faces. Transparent, anti-microbial film oozes out over their uniforms, hardening into a tight seal, allowing only filtered air through. The team that attends to Maj. Gravely's corpse follows suit. Lincoln and Gravely are put onto the same medical thopter; Lincoln is on a med-evac gurney and Gravely is in a body bag. Capt. Fukuwara wants to stay with his co-pilot but is advised against it by a burly Sundarian paramedic. He persists until another paramedic relents. She pins a bio-hazard badge on him and activates it.

The rest of us are escorted by paramedics toward a third thopter. As we trudge across the clearing, Rebecca, Atia, and even Sgt. Jones are visibly shaken and silent. Our ordeal even finally mutes Gen. Alvarez' bluster, although his stern expression betrays nothing of what he truly may be feeling. No one can look each other in the eye, lest one or more of us break down. So instead, I watch the thopter carrying the infected prepare to lift off.

Our ordeal over, the adrenaline drains from my bloodstream, causing the once slow-motion dance of the firefighters to now ramp back up into a frenzied but organized action against the flames now spitting out of our grounded shuttle. With pinpoint proficiency, Sunder's Bravest deploys a cannon which sprays out a white doughy thermal barrier around three sides of the shuttle to prevent any fire from spreading out to the nearby forest. The rest of the fire is reduced to smoldering embers by firefighters using tanks full of a gaseous flame retardant. Our highly advanced EEF shuttle, now a broken, hulking mass, billows thick black smoke into the Sundarian spring sky. The darkened haze rises like a gauze has been pulled up across the Rings.

Even as the smoke pollutes the air, I am transfixed by the the pink 'wall' in the sky that is Sunder's Rings. The spectacular firmament, theoretically the result of some sort of impact which shattered a moon billions of years ago, dazzles like millions of gems dangling overhead. The Sunderian natives are used to the phenomenon, but I'll never be.

As I follow my paramedic across the open field to an awaiting thopter, a great screeching shakes me to attention. A sound as shrill as a rail car braking on top of a herd of feral cats, only louder, pierces my ears.

Rebecca throws up her hands. "What the hell now?"

Firefighters shout electronically altered warnings as they scramble away from the shuttle in all directions. A large wisp of metallic blackness spills out of the hatch onto the grassy clearing like fast moving smoke. The mass rears back high like an untamed horse refusing to be bridled. From side to side, the mass wavers as if examining its surroundings. Dark, smoky tendrils sprout forth like the hair of a Gorgon, lashing out at the firefighters in shiny, black rage.

"My God, what is that thing?" Atia backs away, shielding her eyes from the horror.

I can barely raise my voice above a whisper. "The Dagerites from the cockpit."

"What?" Rebecca asks.

"It's the rest of the Dagerites!"

Rebecca points slowly while backing away. "They can do that? How?"

Looking long and hard at the Dagerites, all I can do is shrug at first. "I don't know. Maybe they're drawing on the metal from the shuttle," I offer.

"That wasn't in your White Paper?" Rebecca asks, keeping her eyes on the steadily growing ball of nanites.

Security forces, who arrived to safeguard the crash site, fire their weapons at the black, metallic swarm. The bullets harmlessly pass through. Quickly, the mass peels away from the smoke like it's shedding skin. Frustrated by security's ineffectiveness, Sgt. Jones removes her service pistol and fires into the swarm. Her bullets penetrate with no resistance also. Small holes seal up in seconds as the Dagerites continue to multiply, possibly feeding off the insides of the shuttle. The loud artificial rattle of the Dagerite swarm sends an unnerving chill all over my body. Confused chatter from the firefighters comes through the comms of every emergency services member. In response, a few firefighters, either brave or foolish, stand their ground and continue to spray the contents of their extinguisher tanks on the shuttle. Some of it splatters onto the dense Dagerite swarm. In a desperate attempt to keep this inorganic beast at bay, two firefighters flank it with a blast of flame retardant directly into its mass. It shrieks and recoils, bringing it in line with three firefighters on its right. They take their turn, shooting the swarm full force with their extinguishers. With a pained artificial cry, the Dagerites disengage and disperse. For a moment I entertain the thought they might be subdued. But they quickly reform once again, with renewed hive-minded vigor, into a great nanite storm cloud.

Never meant as weaponry, the extinguishers appear to be the only thing effective against the Dagerites. But what's in a fire extinguisher that would disrupt a nanite swarm? The firefighters use a combination of the new pressurized foam extinguishers and classic carbon dioxide extinguishers. The only thing they have in common is that they come out cold.

"Cold?" I ask myself aloud.

"What?" Rebecca asks more annoyed than fearful.

"That's it. Cold!" I declare to her.

"Cold?" She grimaces trying to understand my meaning.

"They can't tolerate the cold!" I yell at the firefighters. "Keep spraying it!"

The firefighters nod and press their attack as the contents of their extinguisher tanks slow the Dagerites' advance. With each blast of foamy flame retardant, the swarm recoils in on itself until it forms a giant pulsating sphere of black and silver. Flanked by attacking firefighters, the sphere rolls from side to side in a series of feints to keep them at bay and to avoid the freezing foam. This leaves a wide-open lane at the swarm's front. Whatever intelligence is behind the Dagerites realizes this too. The sphere rolls between the two groups of firefighters right for us: the remaining members of the delegation!

Aiming to finish the job it started on the shuttle; the swarm chitters loudly as if enraged. It gains speed as it barrels toward us, chewing up grass and ground in the process. The collective quickly closes the distance of several dozen meters. Unable to run, Rebecca gulps a bucket of air, leans in close to me, grabs my hand, and squeezes hard. Right in line with its advance, I'm paralyzed before the darting Dagerite sphere. Even though the firefighters pepper and slather the back of the sphere with continued bursts of retardant, it continues to bear down on us.

Should I run? Who am I kidding? I'm not fleet of foot. There is no escape.

The giant sphere dashes forward, overwhelming my field of vision with black and silver. Jagged pulsating dots have joined together in a singular mission of murder: mine. I am about to die, crushed under the weight of the ever-multiplying Dagerite ball. The least I can do is push Rebecca out of the way. I heave to my right, sending the deputy secretary flying. She lands hard a few meters away with a thud and a groan. At least she'll have a chance.

But, only a few meters away from where we stand, the Dagerite sphere shudders to a halt. Atia lets out a tiny squeak like a rat caught in a trap. Even Gen. Alvarez, standing his ground, lets a groan escape. A blanket of frost and foam shrouds the still sphere. Before, its black and silver surface shone with a menacing brilliance. Now the sphere is tarnished and dull like an old heirloom passed down by Death.

Curiosity pushes me forward to see if the monster remains active. Braving both the extreme cold of the flame retardant and possible Dagerite infection, cautious steps take me within an arm's length of the sphere. Foam sloughs off from all sides, leaving huge puddles of white on the park grass. Is it still *alive?* Against my better judgment, I reach out to the sphere praying it won't react.

"Dylan, no!" Rebecca calls out, my fingertips mere millimeters away. "Are you nuts?"

I hold up a single finger for her to stay back.

Trembling, I touch my fingertip to the sphere. The metal is cold from all the flame retardant. The surface is rough from the individual Dagerites joined together. Because of this, I expect the surface to vibrate with activity. Instead, it's as still as a winter night on Pluto. But not for long.

The Dagerite sphere starts to shudder, releasing an indescribable death cry only a non-living thing can originate. Deafening, we are all forced to cover our ears. Since I'm the closest, the cacophony drops me to one knee. The cry subsides into a rustling, like wind blowing through metallic leaves. The sphere quickly loses its shape, falling apart, back into its component Dagerite segments. Like ash, the deactivated Dagerites pile up lifeless on the ground.

My right hand aches. Am I infected? Wait, I didn't touch the sphere with that hand. No, that's not it at all. Rebecca grips my hand as if she intends to cut off all circulation, while grinding my metacarpal bones together. Although dazed, her eyes fill with a glow of appreciation which instantly causes me to become diffident. I look away, tracing an imaginary line from our hands back to the pile of inactive Dagerites.

"Cold? Really?" Rebecca says unaware she's grasping my hand tight.

"So, it would seem," I say pulling my poor hand away from her. "Good to know."

Swallowing hard, I call out to Gen. Alvarez. Standing behind me, he commiserates with a Sunderian security force member cordoning off this area of the park.

"Holy shit, Ambassador!" Alvarez screams, tilting his head toward me at an odd angle and leaning his torso far forward. "Was any of that *swarming* nonsense in the White Paper released by your little subcommittee?"

"Not at all!" I shake some of the feeling back into my hand. "I didn't know about the susceptibility to cold either.

Alvarez cocks an eye.

"I swear, none of this turned up during our investigation."

"Of course not," Alvarez smirks. "You pencil pushers always neglect that last bit of intel we grunts need to operate."

A loud whine cuts off Alvarez before he can read me more of the riot act. Every head snaps to the shuttle. Several of its metal panels are now missing, as if dissolved away, from where the Dagerites must have appropriated it to replicate and form the sphere. Before our eyes, what remains of the left side of the shuttle collapses inward under its own weight with a final crash.

A Sunderian paramedic comes over to us. "I really must insist you come to the hospital for observation. You might be suffering from internal injuries or a concussion and not know it."

Rebecca walks over to one of the medical thopters. "He's right. We should get checked out. Also, I'd like to check on Ken's condition."

The general and I nod with reluctance. The paramedic escorts us to the thopter, along with Atia and Sgt. Jones. After we trudge up the boarding ramp, the pilot beckons us to strap into seats situated against the walls. As the engines engage with a heavy clank and low whir, I'm the last one up the ramp.

But before I board, sounds of a commotion come from the other medical thopter, the one occupied by our infected delegation members and Capt. Fukuwara who went to lend his co-pilot moral support. From my peripheral, Fukuwara and the two-member paramedic team tumble hard out of the back of the hatch and down its ramp to the ground. Their thopter's wings flit as the boarding ramp recedes and the vehicle rises from the ground in spasmodic jerks. The paramedics and Fukuwara writhe in the grass in some sort of distress. As the aircraft gains altitude, Fukuwara jumps up shaking his fists in anger. For several meters, he gives chase across the clearing before surrendering to the futility of such an endeavor.

"Fukuwara, what happened?" I shout, running back down the ramp of our thopter.

He can't hear me. The din of the thopter wings and engine drowns out the swear words the captain lobs skyward.

Sgt. Jones curiously follows me, activating her wrist comm. "Captain! Come in. What happened over there?"

She listens through her earpiece for a few seconds before her brow crumples like paper. "Say that again? Slow down! I can't..." To hear Fukuwara clearer, Jones pushes her earpiece in deep.

"Wait what? Who did that? He did what? Hold on let me put you on speaker!" Jones presses a button on her wrist comm. "Okay Captain, go ahead."

"I said Lt. Lincoln commandeered the medical thopter!" Although Fukuwara's voice is electronically affected, the comm does nothing to mask his panic.

"How?" I squawk back at Jones' wrist. "He was unconscious!"

"Not anymore! He popped straight up like nothing was wrong!" Incredulity replaces the panic in Fukuwara's voice. "Before he even got off the gurney, Lincoln was swinging! He grabbed us like we were little children!"

"And tossed you out the back," I finish. "Yeah, I saw that. Um, what about Gravely? He didn't revive, did he?"

"Thank God, no!" Fukuwara declares. "He's still deader than dead."

Several emergency service workers, including the one who escorted us, and several security force members break off from surveying the shuttle wreckage and rush to help their comrades and Fukuwara.

Rebecca comes bounding back down the ramp. "That's Lincoln up there? How? Where the hell is he going?"

The thopter gets smaller in the distance.

"I've no idea," I say. "But what I do know, is we need to follow. With Lt. Lincoln now under the influence of the Dagerites, no telling what he's planning."

"Pilot!" Gen. Alvarez yells to the cockpit, his clenched fist pulls up his slacks. "Do you see where that other thopter is going?"

"Yes, sir," The Sunderian EMT pilot says over her shoulder.

"Track it and follow! But keep a safe distance."

The pilot, with her green-tinged features and red hair pulled back in a bun, scrutinizes each of her passengers before settling back on Gen. Alvarez' stern expression. "But, sir, this is a medical thopter, not some gunship."

The general purses his lips into a thin line. "I don't care if this meat wagon is a rock and you gotta slingshot us! Follow that thopter!"

The medical pilot can only give an empty gaze, paralyzed by the general's orders. "Uh... sir, I am only... authorized to take you from this accident scene to... uh... Ananda City General Hospital."

Alvarez scowls at the woman with such disdain it's as if she insulted his mother. But before he can read the poor medical pilot the riot act, Fukuwara scrambles into our thopter. Alvarez' scowl slips into a grin.

"We need to go after Lincoln," Fukuwara says strapping himself into a side seat.

Gen. Alvarez gives Fukuwara a long look before he cocks his square head at the medical pilot. "Our thoughts exactly. Why are we still here? We need to fly, Pilot!"

The medical pilot stands up in a weak display of defiance. "I am not authorized to chase other thopters. That's above my pay grade!"

51

Gen. Alvarez looks back at Fukuwara once again. "Captain, your orders are to pursue that hijacked thopter."

Without an afterthought, Fukuwara unbuckles his seatbelt in the back of the medical bay and shimmies past me. He barely acknowledges the medical pilot as he flops into her chair at the controls. Stunned, the Sunderian pilot looks at me as if to ask, 'What should I do?' I have no answers for the poor woman. Protocols on how to deal with infected patients who hijack thopters don't exist. I swear the green of her skin pales as if she's nauseous from the pressure Gen. Alvarez has exerted on her.

"I'm sorry." It's all I can offer as my stomach quivers when I'm caught in her desperate gaze. I grab a quick glance at her name tag. "EMT Bose is it?"

Overwhelmed, the medical pilot perks up at the sound of her own name with just enough wherewithal to nod her head.

"EMT Bose, I promise we will return this thopter back to you in one piece. Won't we, Capt. Fukuwara?"

EMT Bose locks eyes with Fukuwara for a moment before he smiles and pats the paramedic on the arm with a tad bit of condescension. She's fairly dumbstruck by it all; the protest in her all but gone.

Alvarez stands to the side of the pilot, draping his arm around her like an old friend. And like an expert ballroom dancer, the general leads the medical pilot away from the cockpit and to the ramp. With a polite shove, he releases the confused EMT at the bottom of the ramp. "Sorry ma'am, the EEF requires this thopter to remedy an emergency galactic incident." With a deft flourish, Alvarez spins on his heels. "Captain Fukuwara, take us up!"

"Sir, yes sir!" Fukuwara buckles up, switching from passenger to pilot without question.

Rebecca, Atia, Sgt. Jones, and I all give Gen. Alvarez the side eye. He notices. "Hey, it's called 'commandeering an aircraft,' people! I'm legally authorized to do so."

I buckle my seatbelt. "Um, thank you. I guess?"

The thopter's engines whine in anticipation of giving chase. Alvarez sits up front with Fukuwara and tries to get eyes on the fleeing thopter. Atia gleefully buckles into a seat next to Sgt. Jones. Rebecca takes the seat next to me.

Alvarez looks back and shakes his head with stiff resolve. "No, no, no! Deputy Secretary French, you and Miss Watkins need to deplane now!"

"Wait, what?" Rebecca asks. "Why does Ambassador Dylan get to stay?

Alvarez slings an arm over the back of his chair, not at all bothered by her resistance to leaving. "Because Mr. Ambassador is the only one here who knows about those *Dager-y* things. I need his intel and his insight."

"Atia, you are not coming." I point back down the ramp, finding it unbelievable the general and myself agree on something. "Uh, sorry Rebecca — I mean Deputy Secretary. You really shouldn't come."

Atia's mouth is agape as if I've betrayed her. "On diplomatic missions, I go where you go, Boss. You know that."

I hate it when she calls me 'Boss.'

"Listen here, Mr. Ambassador!" Rebecca says. She would jump out of her seat if she wasn't already strapped in. "I'm the Deputy Secretary of State here on behalf of Earth-Gov to organize this peace process and I'm seeing these Ananda Accords through to the bitter end. If it means chasing a nanite-infected freak halfway across Sunder, that's what I'm going to do! Don't forget. I'm the ranking member of this delegation."

"Oh great!" Alvarez growls at the pulling of rank. "It's a damn party boat!"

Sgt. Jones simply shrugs as she buckles herself into her seat. She is a soldier after all. The good ones know how to suck it up, go with the flow, and endure when the situation is in constant flux. With a sigh and an eye roll, I decide to resign myself to the ever-changing situation as well and buckle up. I can only hope Rebecca and Atia can stay out of harm's way. That *harm* is something I should have made sure was handled years ago. I should have remained vigilant, like a hawk, with each and every tiny machine and had them smashed like the bugs they are.

The ramp rises with the close of the medi-thopter's rear doors. With a loud clank, the automatic locks secure us from the devastation outside. Our commandeered thopter leaps off the ground like a mechanized rabbit. The thopter accelerates forward with a powerful thrust, and for a moment pins us to our seats. My stomach sinks against my spine. Breakfast feels like it's in my chest.

Chapter Five

The flight is smoother than expected. Rocket jocks like Fukuwara can fly just about anything. The serenity of the purplish-pink sky fills the windscreen of the thopter, deceiving me into believing that all is right with the universe. But I know otherwise.

"Come on, come on," Rebecca grunts through gritted teeth. She fumbles with her mobile, giving it several violent shakes. She jabs at the cracked screen, willing the device back to life with muttered curses.

"What's wrong?" I ask.

Her nose wrinkles upward. "We need to contact the State Department. My mobile is damaged. Some of the apps are off-line."

I consider how this incident could be perceived. "That could be a good thing. You might want to hold off for a bit."

"*Could* be a good thing?" She cocks one smoky eye at me. "How so? Earth is under attack!"

"How is Earth under attack?" Atia asks from across the table where a patient would be attended to.

I let out a heavy sigh that has built up in my chest since the crash.

"We are the official representation of Earth. This delegation being attacked is the same as Earth being attacked."

"That's right." Rebecca shakes her mobile at Atia. "This is a declaration of war which needs a swift response; that's why the secretary of state and the president need to know ASAP."

She's starting to sound like Alvarez.

"We know what we're up against — the Dagerites." I tell her in an attempt to tamp down her ire. "But we don't know who sent them."

"My best guess is the Adamahn." Alvarez blurts out over his shoulder.

"We don't know that, General." I say before turning to Rebecca for another pass at convincing her of the same. "Before looking for blame, let's stop what's in front of us first. The people of Sunder are in serious danger."

"I spoke with the Sunderian security forces while we were on the ground," Alvarez says. "They are on high alert concerning the Adamahn."

Rebecca's sobering stare pierces deep, searching for something within me she can hang her trust on. "Fine, I'll keep Earth updated without judgments on who hit us."

I thank her with a quick two-fingered salute.

"Remember this, Ambassador," she continues forthright. "The leash — it's a short one." Her warning sends a slight shiver through me.

Gen. Alvarez waves his beefy hand at the cockpit control panel. "Does this meat wagon have the means to track that other medi-thopter?"

Fukuwara points at a monitor near his knee. "Yes sir, these sensors here help keep track of their entire emergency fleet." With his calm demeanor, I can tell this is not the captain's first hot pursuit.

"Is that the other thopter?" Alvarez points at what I can only make out as a blip on the screen.

"Yes, sir."

"Well? Get after that son of a bitch! Go! Go!" Alvarez rages at the cockpit windscreen.

The thopter banks hard right, gaining altitude as it rises over a large neon-green hill. As Fukuwara slides his fingers along an LED touch pad, the thopter accelerates and pushes us back further in our seats. Beyond the windscreen, the mammoth skyscrapers of Ananda-proper come into view.

"He's going to get away!" Alvarez throws back his head. "Can't you make this thing go faster? Do people routinely die in these slow-assed meatbuckets? Come on man, faster!"

Fukuwara's hand gives the slightest tremble, so I decide to intercede. "Give him a break, General. Let him get accustomed to the vehicle."

Alvarez twists like a corkscrew in his seat. "First off, this is a military op now, and second, I'll give the captain a break when the mission is accomplished, *Ambassador*!"

"Hounding Fukuwara is not helping, *General*! Wherever we're going, I would prefer to get there in one piece."

Fukuwara's hands steady at my magic words.

Alvarez swivels his seat back toward the windscreen with a hard jerk. "This is a military op now," he repeats, his words deliberate and calm. "You, Ambassador Dylan, are merely the expert on all things Dagerite. Otherwise, I'd throw..."

"General! Mr. Ambassador!" Fukuwara slams his palm on the control panel. "If I may speak freely."

"You may." Suspicion tinges the general's voice.

"I wasn't always a glorified chauffeur, you know," Fukuwara says. "I flew combat for five years! I've got this."

Alvarez glares at him for at least forever, but says nothing, leaving a permanent scowl etched on his face.

For several minutes, we fly in silence, all eyes following the on-screen blip that is the elusive Lt. Lincoln. Silence hangs heavy until Gen. Alvarez cries out, "Is that him?"

Frantic, he points at the glass with one hand and claps Fukuwara on the back with the other. A red speck floats against the purple and pink sky in a spasmodic pattern.

Fukuwara's eyes light up. "I've got a visual on Lincoln!"

"Stay with him, Captain." Alvarez barks the command with more encouragement than bluster.

The errant medi-thopter grows larger weaving through the air with erratic yaws and fitful dips toward the spires of Ananda as we close in on it. Though safe to assume that an uninfected Lt. Lincoln was once a seasoned pilot like Fukuwara, under the influence of a malevolent power, he's not up to speed with controlling his thopter.

Rubbing his hands on his thighs, Alvarez sits tall in his chair. "Can you catch him?"

Without turning to the general, Fukuwara narrows his focus on the medi-thopter, now at his twelve o'clock, before answering. "This meat-wagon can't maneuver as well as the Osprey-39s I flew at Salsola. But back in the day, I chased Pallid-class Harriers on a regular."

"What does that mean?" Rebecca asks.

Fukuwara flashes a boyish grin. "It means I can catch him."

The captain slides the acceleration faders forward. The surprising jolt of momentum pushes us all backward. Only Sgt. Jones sits unfazed. She rides out the sudden acceleration with an actual grin while the rest of us tighten not only our seatbelts but certain unnamed orifices. Our medi-thopter remains on Lincoln's six, steadily closing in.

"Flank him!" Gen. Alvarez' voice booms above the engine roar.

"Copy that!" Fukuwara responds. The two men are in their element. The captain yanks the stick to the right and forward causing the thopter to lurch in those directions. And just like that we are sidled up alongside the stolen thopter. My stomach catches up a moment later.

Gen. Alvarez scans the control panel. "Can this meat wagon talk to that one?"

Sgt. Jones perks up. "Yes sir! Punch up 2-0-1 on the comm-link. That should be the Sunderian emergency services channel." She looks at her wrist comm once again. "Scans tell me the thopter's call signal is 0-7-9-4."

Alvarez punches in the numbers on the comm. A low trill rings out from the speaker signaling a connection has been made. "Lt. Lincoln! Come in Lt. Lincoln! This is Gen. Alvarez!" There is no answer. "Dammit Lincoln, I know you hear me!"

"Lincoln's not here." The voice that replies over the comms is playful and calm. Although it is electronically affected, Lincoln's voice now has that same strange hollowness that was in Maj. Gravely's voice.

"Whoever the hell you are, you land that thopter now! That's an order!" Alvarez barks.

"I don't take orders from you, General." Lincoln snarls through the comms like he's offended by the order's pointlessness.

Alvarez is unperturbed and barks back. "Fine! Who do you take orders from and where do you think you're going to go, Lieutenant? You'll find no sanctuary in Ananda City or anywhere else on Sunder!"

"I don't seek sanctuary." Lincoln scoffs at the assumption like a petulant child. "I've got a new mission, General."

Lincoln's comm channel goes dead.

Without warning, his thopter veers right at us. Thankfully, Fukuwara pulls the stick right and back to avoid being side-swiped. Everyone is jerked around in our seats, causing Atia to let out another tiny squeak. Thank God, he reacted in time.

From my side window, Lincoln's aircraft accelerates and flies right into the heart of the city, cutting between buildings without a care for those structures or his life. In order to stay on his tail, we too descend into Ananda, now an obstacle course of concrete, steel and glass. We follow the hijacked aircraft into a steep dive. My lungs push up into my chest, making my next breath difficult. We drop in altitude low enough for Sunderians on the ground to take notice. Walkers, workers, and wide-eyed bystanders, point upward from their daily tasks. They gesticulate at the harrowing spectacle we must appear to them. Perceptive enough to not send us hurtling into the deck, Fukuwara pitches the thopter upward with several tugs on the stick, keeping us above the rooftops. Abruptly, our thopter pitches left. Its flapping wings miss a building's outcropping by the narrowest of margins. My stomach turns over when the captain performs an abrupt yaw maneuver to evade an onrushing facade. Before I can release the air trapped in my lungs, another building appears out of nowhere. The glare of burnished steel and glass fills the entire windscreen. Fukuwara makes a hard bank around it and I swear my insides shift out of place.

In the back, Atia's knees are far into her chest as if she wants to climb into herself and be somewhere else. Rebecca's eyes are wired shut. She grips my arm tight, regardless of my waning courage. There is little comfort I can give her right now. All the while, Sgt. Jones simply sits back rocking in her seat, eyes calm and focused. Not sure if it is the shaking of the thopter or my stress, but I swear she still has that slight smile on her face. I put my head in my hands, unable to watch. All that's left for me to do right now is try to endure the tossing, turning, rising, dipping, and dropping.

"Watch it, Captain!" Alvarez shouts.

I lift my head in time to see Gen. Alvarez shake Fukuwara by the shoulder. "Watch those buildings coming up!"

Fukuwara shrugs off Alvarez like he's a persistent bee and not his anxious superior. "I see it! Can't miss it."

The buildings they speak of I recognize. "That's the Archive Tower Complex!"

Looming across the horizon like a mountain range of brilliant steel and glass, the Archive Tower Complex ominously fills our view with its massive buildings. Interconnected structures ascending far into the late afternoon sky, threaten to swat down both thopters as we fly ever closer.

"Oh my God, the Archive Tower?" Rebecca shrinks inward. "He's going to crash into it! We're supposed to visit there tomorrow and he's going to crash into it!"

Fukuwara cranes his short neck along the windscreen. "No, wait look! Lincoln's landing!"

The hijacked thopter corkscrews down out of view between two buildings within the complex. Fukuwara is too close to follow suit. He circles wide, swinging back, then descends. Our view through the windscreen shows that Lincoln has made a rough landing amidst scattering pedestrians and workers in the Archive Tower's paved plaza. One of its skiffs broken, the thopter lists on its right side. Smoke billows out from underneath.

Gen. Alvarez bounces in his seat. "Land, land, land!"

Fukuwara flips switches. "Roger that, sir. But I have to hover and find a good landing area. Can't go squashing civilians."

We descend and circle above the plaza, once, twice, three times. My stomach spins with each loop. Thankfully, breakfast stays settled inside me, but precious time is lost.

"Right there!" Alvarez spots an opening in a corner of the plaza, in front of a smaller support building where there are fewer panicked pedestrians.

"Roger that!" Fukuwara presses a button, and the landing gear engages with a droning whine. He pulls back on control sliders, taking us into a fairly rapid vertical descent that pushes my guts into my diaphragm. We land with a hard bounce, settling into place after a few skips across the cement. Atia lets out another one of her squeaks. When she realizes this is not a crash landing, she checks the cabin sheepishly for witnesses.

Outside, is a chaotic scene. People with green pallid faces stumble and scatter in all directions. Shrill voices call out for help as Sunderians and Outworlders give both thopters wide berths. Lincoln stands out from the throng. Calm as a tomb, he heads for the Archive Tower's main building. His movements, though rigid, are still surprisingly swift. In the process of entering the glass doors of the lobby, he knocks several panicked Sunderian locals to the ground.

The captain flips switches that shut down the wings and engine, prepping it for us to deplane.

"Why the hell is he going in there?" Rebecca says, mouth agape, as she quickly unbuckles her safety belt.

"Who cares! Probably wants hostages." Gen. Alvarez blurts, already unbuckled and stomping his way toward the lowering ramp. "Jones, you still got ammo in your service weapon?"

"Sir, yes, sir!" She says with a gleam in her eye, jumping out of her seat like someone set her on fire.

Alvarez turns on a dime with Sgt. Jones in tow, pistol at the ready. "Good! Let's put that *thing* down before it does more damage!"

Rebecca whips around to me in the cramped confines of the medi-thopter, nearly knocking into me with her athletic frame. "What could Lincoln possibly want in the Archive Tower, Dylan?"

Unbuckling my safety belt, I stand feeling a little weak-kneed, but my mind is strong and alert. "The Dagerites' primary purpose is to overwrite computer systems. What is the Archive Tower, but the largest computerized Hall of Records not only for Sunder, but for much of the galaxy."

"It's so much more than that." Atia springs from her seat like a young sprite with renewed vigor, finally finding her voice. "The Archive Tower is one big data repository for governments, multi-planetary corporations and super rich private citizens with something to hide!"

Rebecca's eyes spark with alertness. "Do you think Lincoln or Gravely *knew* to come here?"

"Yes! *Whoever* is controlling Lincoln *had* to have the infection of this place as part of their plans. Our deaths would have been major news and would have provided the perfect distraction. Since he was the first to be infected, I believe the major was supposed to survive the crash."

"Exactly," Atia says making her way down the ramp. "Our lives in exchange for an entire galaxy's worth of data."

Five years ago, the government subcommittee sessions on the Dagerites were closed to the public and press. We considered the biggest threat of the Dagerites being an uncontrolled outbreak on a moonbase, or maybe the damn things running rampant on a small rebellious planet out in the Reach. How small-minded we were. Our thinking wasn't creative enough to imagine that someone could use the Dagerites to try and *control* the galaxy. We didn't think creatively because all we cared about was covering it all up and covering our asses for signing off on such a dangerous defense project. The political will to *solve* the problem was sorely lacking in that subcommittee, lacking in me.

Unable to change the past, but desperate to prevent a mindless future, I start down the ramp. "Are you coming, Deputy Secretary?"

Rebecca gives it a thought for only a moment, before vaulting down the ramp, her heels tapping out loud in enthusiastic clanks. "I'm in. It's a bit difficult to expose megalomaniacs from behind a desk?"

Chapter Six

Like terrified ants fleeing a damaged hill, Sunderians stream from the main building of the Archive Tower into the plaza. Way ahead of us, Gen. Alvarez and Sgt. Jones wade through the fleeing pedestrians, staff, and technicians following Lincoln's path of mayhem. With our group now split in two, Fukuwara takes the lead as he attempts to reach his 'possessed' co-pilot, paying little attention to the frightened Sunderians around him. Plowing through the panicked throng is like swimming upstream. Twice, the crush sweeps Atia back. I yank her through the rabble like a fretful child. Determined not to be separated, Rebecca vice-grips my shoulder. The constant knocks and bumps from the on-rushers help me ignore the pain. The closer we get to the entrance, the more determined Fukuwara is to get inside. Focused on confronting what once was his best friend and colleague, he has forgotten Rebecca, Atia, and myself. He clears a path with strong enough shoves to send staff members and tourists reeling.

But what will he do once he does reach Lincoln? For my own safety, I need to know. I'll need to keep an eye on him, or he might get his damn foolish-self killed, infected, or worse, get one of us infected.

Inside the lobby, Lt. Lincoln scuffles with security. He gets the best of them by tossing the red blazer-wearing security personnel around like trash. From a distance, I make out something shaped like a dark spear swiftly extending out from Lincoln. Whatever it is makes hard contact with one of the guards. The man goes limp and drops out of view behind the front reception desk. Lincoln does something with his hands behind the desk, before he briskly walks around a corner to the elevator banks. He's quickly chased by Gen. Alvarez, Sgt. Jones and a handful of guards. I want to lend aid, but we have our own problems right now with trying not to not get trampled by this terrified crowd.

Above the din of confusion, the klaxon call of the building's alarm system blares out into the plaza through the open glass doors. With the alarm activated, the automatic doors slowly slide closed. Lockdown protocols are going into effect.

"No, no, no!" I shout ahead. "Fukuwara! Stop those doors!"

As a scared staff member scampers out, Fukuwara rushes up and shoves his body between the lobby doors. He gets a good handhold and pushes them back, holding them open in the way the biblical Samson might have pushed against the pillars of old Temple Dagon. Quickly, I duck underneath his armpit into the lobby. Rebecca is right behind me. Atia finally frees herself from the crush of fleeing bystanders but is still a few meters away from the doors.

"Come on, Atia!" I egg her on.

Fukuwara's body trembles as he struggles against the doors' singular drive to close. The thick glass double doors grind in place within their tracks as I reach out and pull Atia inside underneath the captain's arms. Unlike Samson, Fukuwara lacks the strength to bring the doors down all together. Instead, he lunges forward into the lobby and the glass doors slam shut behind him with a whooshing thump. Out in the plaza, a squad of armed security guards make their way through the crowd toward the entrance as a titanium gate rolls down. It's too late for them. The doors will remain closed unless someone within deactivates lockdown.

Inside, the security alarm sounds a deafening clangor that ricochets off the marble floor and walls of the lobby. The bulk of the staff has gone. Either they've managed to escape before lockdown, or they are hunkered down in place.

"Doesn't the Archive Tower have more security teams?" Rebecca stares dumbfounded at the long, unmanned security desk. "And what about the general and Sgt. Jones, where'd they go off to?"

"I saw them," I say. "They were with the rest of the guards who left this station in pursuit of Lincoln."

Atia grabs my arm as she listens to the security squad attempt to breach the doors. "How strong are their safeguards against hacks? You know, are their contingency plans up to snuff?"

"Contingency plans within contingency plans. And that's on top of the best cyber-security." I try not to sound worried about the security team's absence in the lobby.

Rebecca shakes her head, still not convinced. "I bet these Tower officials never dreamed of this."

They didn't, but *I should have dreamed of this* in that damned Senate hearing.

The lobby of the Archive Tower is massive. The cavernous splendor of the Tower lobby's artwork and architecture slow the pace of Rebecca and Atia. They can't help but take a moment and drink it all in. Brilliant white walls, columns, and floors of marble, so smooth and clean you can almost make out your own reflection. In the center of the floor, a large inlay of a logo cast in brass, depicts an ancient scribe recording Sunder's first bits of worthwhile information onto a stone tablet.

"Whoa!" Atia says, staring toward the high ceiling at a mosaic depicting the first library on Sunder. It was once located on this very site. The masterwork of the mosaic provides the lobby's only splash of color with its square bits of green, pink and yellow. But the staccato blare of the alarms, echoing off every pristine surface, brings her back to reality.

Meanwhile, Rebecca remains enthralled by the gigantic reliefs lining the back wall of the lobby. These depict Sunder's early librarians safeguarding ancient scrolls. The reliefs emerge from the walls as a welcome reminder of the Tower's illustrious history and duty. Today, these carvings stand as pale harbingers of what is at stake within.

Although my first visit to the Archive Tower Complex was four years ago, the first of several, I'm still impressed by the gilded images and acknowledgments to history all the artwork depicts. Unfortunately, there's no time to waste on fully appreciating it all, so I slip around the security desk to access the lobby's security computer and to check the monitors. Rebecca and Fukuwara follow.

I freeze in my tracks. In the rush, Fukuwara bumps into me. Together we pause at the sight of a Sunderian guard, dead, seated on the floor and propped up against the wall. Blood splatters the wall behind the guard's head.

"Dear God," Rebecca whispers.

Atia hoists half her short torso over the desk to get a peek at the security computer but sees what we have discovered. "Is he..."

"Dead? Yes." I'm unable to turn away.

"They must have threatened Lincoln," Fukuwara stutters. "He's gotta be scared at this point."

"Riiiight." Rebecca sneers at Fukuwara.

The computer terminal above the poor soul has Dagerites crawling all over it. Damaged beyond repair, any sort of input has been prevented. But two sets of security monitors next to the computer still function.

Atia comes around to the other side of the security desk. "Lincoln must have tried infecting this place through this terminal. Luckily, the security system and the data system are separate for situations like this. All he managed to do was plunge this place into lockdown."

"How do you know the systems are separate?" I ask, even though I'm sure I already know.

Atia refuses to meet my gaze. "Let's say I did some deep research for our visit."

"I have an idea," I announce to the group. "Rebecca, you and the captain watch that left bank of monitors for Lincoln. Atia and I will check these on the right."

The monitors reveal almost every nook and cranny of the Tower that isn't a restroom. On one monitor, a Sunderian woman and man have hunkered down by a desk in their office. The woman is furiously writing something, while the man is speaking fast into his mobile. On another monitor, an Earther man hides under his desk. His head is tilted, listening for imminent rescue. And on yet another monitor, a young Sunderian woman frantically waves at her window. My educated guess is she's trying to get the attention of the security squad that's locked out in the plaza. We survey the monitors for several minutes in silence. The only sound comes from outside. The security team bangs against the gate trying to find ways to enter, but to no avail.

"Look there!" The Deputy Secretary blurts out.

"Where?" I slide over to her side of the security desk as an anxious Fukuwara peers over her shoulder.

"There!" She points. "On level 68! Lincoln's taking on more security guards."

On the small monitor, Lt. Lincoln punches, kicks, and flips guards over his shoulder. Before I can formulate a response, Fukuwara darts around the corner to the elevator banks. I give chase.

"Fukuwara, wait! We shouldn't get separated! We need a plan!"

There are six elevators within this set of elevator banks. Only one is active. The other five have come down to the lobby and gone dark as part of lockdown protocols. Repeatedly, Fukuwara pokes at the active elevator's button, focusing only on its red glow.

"We've got to get to Lincoln before the general and Jones do," he says.

"Agreed," I reply.

"They don't know him. They'll just kill him!"

"I won't let that happen."

"Lincoln's a good man," Fukuwara continues without a beat. "Back home, he's got a girl and a family who love him. He's not himself. He's confused, is all! He doesn't deserve to be shot down like some glow-slug!"

When I was a small child, I didn't have a ton of friends. So, loyalty is something I deeply respect. Unfortunately, Lincoln is likely a lost cause. No one has ever returned to normal after a Dagerite infection, and that was if they survived. But Fukuwara's eyes are so pained. I don't have the power to be blunt with the captain, but I do not want to sugarcoat his co-pilot's predicament either. For now, I decide to remain silent.

Rebecca double-times it to the elevator banks as if she's ready for anything. "I didn't see Gen. Alvarez and Sgt. Jones on the monitors."

The elevator doors slide open, and I wave everyone aboard. "Follow the sounds of mayhem. I'm sure they'll be with Tower security. Level 68, please."

"Level 68," responds the elevator's artificial male voice in a deep and sanguine tone. The doors close and we speed upward with minute inertial resistance.

"What's the plan?" Rebecca asks. "What's to stop the Dagerites from getting into the Tower's data systems?" Her hazel eyes, full of worry, shimmer in the elevator's fluorescence.

Before I can answer, my stomach flutters when her pupils cast my reflection back at me. "Um, first we reunite with Alvarez and Jones. Afterward, we find the master archivist."

"Master archivist? Do you think civilians are still in the facility?"

"Civilians are still here. Saw them on the lobby monitors. Besides, the master archivist would never leave his post. I can fill him in about the Dagerites. And Atia can use her coding skills to help with any remaining archivists to create firewalls that might keep the critters out." I turn to Atia. "You think you're up for this?"

"Come on, Boss!" She puts one slender hand on her petite hip and holds out the other in a small fist. "Remember that situation with King Dodi? I still got it."

Atia knows I hate it when she calls me 'Boss,' but I fist-bump her anyway.

"Wait!" Rebecca crosses her arms and leans in. "What 'King Dodi situation?'"

Atia sticks out her chin and raises one expertly plucked eyebrow. "I *dug up* information on King Dodi so the Ambassador could schmooze the pants, or whatever the hell that crazy outfit he wears, off of him."

Rebecca backs away to the other side of the small elevator. "You hacked King Dodi for the Lyca Summit?"

Atia crosses her arms sporting a mischievous grin.

"Dear God!" Rebecca covers her eyes. "That's terrible! That's criminal!"

Atia, leans against the elevator wall, wearing her confidence like a crown. Her face is a mask of false atonement. "King Dodi is Earth's best friend now, right?"

Rebecca blinks at her, then turns to me. "And you approved of this?

My sheepish smirk is apparent. "King Dodi was so inscrutable. We needed an angle. Diplomacy by any means necessary, right? That's what *our* boss told me. The President didn't seem to mind."

Rebecca's eyes, bright and wide, roll back into her head. "That can never get out. Understand?"

"Would never dream of it, Deputy Secretary." I turn to the LCD floor indicator and watch the numbers ascend.

"So, what's the second part of the plan?" Rebecca says, ready to move the topic away from hacking heads of state.

"We should try to recreate what the firefighters accomplished in the park."

"Freeze Lincoln?" Rebecca jumps at the idea like a schoolchild who knows she has the correct answer.

"After a fashion," I say, trying not to look at Fukuwara. "This building is not only up to code, but if I remember from my last tour here, it should be beyond what's required. The sprinkler system should be equipped with cold foam, there should be cold extinguishers throughout the building, and of course, there's omni-thermostat control."

"That's good." Rebecca says. "We trap him and maybe get him cold enough, so the Dagerites die in his body."

That's wishful thinking, but I keep quiet out of respect for Fukuwara who silently broods in his own corner of the elevator.

"We'll do the best we can to help him," I muster.

In silence, we ride the rest of the way, anxiously eying the floor numbers tick upward. Each digit change strikes with every throb in my chest.

Chapter Seven

Our arrival to the 68th floor is signified by a soft dinging sound and the electronic voice's happy announcement. When the doors finally open, Fukuwara rushes out first, spinning around in the hallway, directionless.

"If the general and the sergeant haven't gotten to Lincoln yet, let me try to reason with him face to face first," he says after we exit the elevator.

I acquiesce with my silence.

To our left, we hear shouts and chatter, so we rush in that direction. Rectangular fluorescent lights spray cones of illumination every three meters or so along the extensive hallway. The smooth floor is the same color as the walls, a dull muted ivory. Running along the length of the ceiling is a thick steel pipe. Smaller pipes branch off from it at five-meter intervals and snake through the walls into the countless data center areas behind them. From my last visit here, I remember the pipe's purpose is to carry cold air, from massive cooling units located at the rear of the Archive Tower, to every data stack inside in order to prevent them from overheating, but not too much as to cause the storage units to freeze. Even the smaller buildings have a version of this setup. Whoever is controlling Lincoln, do they intend to take control of the facility, or sabotage it?

The closer we get to the sounds of activity along this stretch of hallway, the lower the temperature drops. My mouth and throat become dry from the lack of moisture in the air. Rebecca rubs her arms as she jogs, while Atia shivers, letting out a few 'brrr' sounds along the way. Meanwhile, Fukuwara shows no signs of discomfort. As a soldier, he knows how to push through a mere change in climate. He focuses only on the task at hand: finding and helping his friend.

The hallway widens out into a large, utilitarian reception area for one of the major data stacks. Across from reception is a double-doored glass entrance. On the glass, depicted in LCD lights, are the words 'Data Stack B'. The bold, authoritative letters scroll across in a looping horizontal march. There we find Gen. Alvarez and Sgt. Jones peering through the pristine glass, like wanting children in front of a toy store. They've managed to muster about ten members of the Tower's security personnel, which is oddly made up of mostly Earthers and only a few Sunderians. While the team sets up barricades, three Earther security guards are seated on the smooth floor, attending to their relatively minor wounds. Fukuwara approaches Sgt. Jones, and they huddle together in conversation.

Beyond the doors, rows and rows of computer terminals blink with activity. Usually, they're manned by attentive Sunderians, whose glassy green eyes monitor the steady flow of data into the system. These trusted observers, known as archivists, are nowhere to be found, leaving the data stack vulnerable.

Away from the security team, on the other side of the reception area, stands a lone Sunderian archivist. Dressed in his white two-piece archivist uniform, he runs a shaky hand through his gray hair. His narrow green eyes dart from one area beyond the Data Stack glass to another. As he paces back and forth, a sheen of sweat on his forehead glistens in the fluorescence.

"What's the situation, General?" I ask, sidling up to Alvarez. He looks content now that he has someone else's automatic weapon in his hand.

He flinches at my presence, pointing the gun in my direction. "Jeez Ambassador, I thought you diplomats caught a bus back to the Concorde already."

I hold up my hands in mock surrender. "Soon General, soon. But let's put the Dagerites to bed first."

Alvarez jerks a thumb back at the glass. "Lt. Lincoln is holed up in that Data Stack. The archivist over there thinks he's trying to get into a *clean room* or something."

"Clean room? What's that?" Rebecca asks.

Clearing his throat, the short Sunderian finally steps over to our side of the reception area. "The Clean Room Vaults are where we keep many of the drives, discs, servers, films and crystals used in our data stack system. The rooms have to be kept spotless so as not to contaminate the storage devices, hence the name. And that man in there not only assaults my personnel, but risks contamination of Data Stack B!"

Rebecca squints at him. "And you are?"

"I, madam, am Master Archivist Phaleron. Demetrio Phaleron." He adjusts the yellow master's sash hanging across his uniform. "I cannot believe all of the other archivists have fled. Protecting data is our sworn duty."

Even though the stack is now vulnerable to attack, I don't blame any of the archivists for abandoning their posts amid the deadly chaos Lincoln has wrought.

"Mr. Phaleron, I'm Rebecca French, Deputy Secretary of State for Earth-Gov. And this is Earth's Ambassador to the United Order of Planets, DeMarco Dylan."

"Oh, I know Ambassador Dylan well." Phaleron manages a smile. "We have met on other official visits to the Archive Tower. It is a shame we are reunited again under such circumstances."

We shake hands. "Still, it's good to see you again, Master Archivist. I take it General Alvarez has filled you in on our situation?"

Alvarez stops talking to a member of the security team to answer. "I filled him in on as much as I understand. *You're* the expert on these nanites."

The backhanded compliment makes me bristle.

Phaleron shakes his head. "Nanites infecting both machine *and* living tissue. That is ..." He can't find the words. For the uninitiated, this is understandable.

"I was speechless myself," Rebecca says. "But rest assured, Master Phaleron, Sunder has the full support of Earth-Gov in handling this matter."

"Gratitudes, Deputy Secretary." Phaleron leans into a curt bow. His dimpled smile allows his handsome features to shine through his worry.

"How come the defenses for the complex aren't fully automated?" Rebecca asks.

Phaleron raises his chin high and throws back his shoulders. "Deputy Secretary, we here on Sunder appreciate our history of *personally* protecting the information and chronicles of our clients. No matter the technological advancements aiding our endeavors, we believe the humanoid touch should always be a dominating constant."

"I see." Rebecca straightens, impressed.

"Such a shame," he continues. "You were supposed to visit our humble facility *tomorrow* when we would have put our best foot forward."

Rebecca returns the smile. "I'm certain your hospitality is top-notch. Unfortunately, the man holed up inside that Clean Room forced a change in our schedule."

Phaleron places a hand over his heart. "The general told me you all were in an accident earlier. By the Burning Scrolls, why are you people not in a hospital?"

Rebecca waves away his concerns. "Long story, Master Archivist. What's important now is that we aid you in any way possible."

Phaleron's eyes light up. "Oh gratitudes! We were waiting for the mobile security team to arrive."

"Mobile security?" Rebecca asks.

The Master Archivist becomes more animated and begins talking with his hands. "Each data stack has its own security team. But the mobile team provides security for the grounds of the complex and can quickly mobilize to backup any one of the data stack's security."

"Bad news, Master Phaleron." I purse my lips and meet his green-eyed stare. "We saw the mobile team and I don't think they're coming. They couldn't get in the building before lockdown went into effect."

"Oh dear." Phaleron rubs his hands together. "It will be hours before they can decrypt the commands to deactivate lockdown from the outside. With my credentials, I can deactivate them from the inside, but only with the aid of a chief archivist working together in sync."

"And where is this chief archivist?" I ask.

"Chief Archivist Barrera was inside Data Stack B the last time I saw him." Phaleron takes one anxious step toward the data stack door. "My chief archivist would never leave his post during an emergency alarm."

"No worries, Master Archivist." Rebecca's says with a reassuring smile. "We *will* find your chief and stop our man's attack."

Gen. Alvarez straightens, slings his borrowed automatic rifle behind his back, and leans in. "And how do *you* plan on stopping Lincoln, Deputy Secretary?"

Rebecca shrinks from the general. "I mean, Dylan has a way that might work. Which I support. Right Ambassador?"

"I do?" I lean away, not appreciating being put on the spot like this. "Um, yes — I do."

Phaleron turns to me, his face pleading. "You say you can stop him without doing damage to the data stack. But that man came in here like a juggernaut — he seemed possessed!"

"In a sense, he is." I confirm. "But I have an idea that might contain him. It proved effective earlier."

I explain to Phaleron our ordeal in the park and how the firefighters used cold extinguishers and foam to affect the Dagerites. When I finish, Phaleron takes a half step back, rubbing his gray goatee. "By the Burning Scrolls!"

Rebecca steps next to me and places a hand on my shoulder in support of my claims. I swallow hard. Am I worthy of her faith? A slight wave of nausea comes over me as I'm unable to shake the memory of that day of the secret senate hearings. Filled with such hubris, we members of the subcommittee believed we had it all sorted out. Shut down the Dagerite debacle quickly and quietly; the public need not know a thing. That was our biggest concern. We hoped it would all go away like it never existed. But we should have made certain, by bearing witness to the destruction of all core samples, burning the design specs, and atomizing whatever was left. Instead, we — *I mean I* — out of political expediency, encouraged the subcommittee to trust one shell corporation after another to bury the mess. In the fast-paced world of defense contracting, lack of accountability and ethics are the name of the game. I should have known better.

The feverish gaze in Phaleron's eyes beats back the heaviness in my chest. So, I open up about an assumption now nagging me. "Master Phaleron, I think Lt. Lincoln is compelled by an unknown agent to come to the Archive and *deliberately* infect the system."

Phaleron wrings his hands while glaring through the glass doors. "Data Stack B, like all the other Data Stacks, connects to the Hub, the master archive! It's located underground. This Lincoln fellow would never have access to that. He doesn't need to. Because if he infects this data stack, the corruption will spread to the Hub and out to the other five Data Stacks!"

"I understand Master Phaleron, but —"

"The data, the histories, the ideas of a hundred billion souls from a myriad of worlds would be lost forever!" Phaleron throws his hands up in frustration.

"Master Phaleron, I don't think the plan is destruction," I try to explain. "Information is power as they say. What if this attack was about control?"

"That's just great," Rebecca says, swatting the air. "Whoever tried to assassinate our delegation used it as cover for *this* attack."

"By the Burning Scrolls, such madness! Sophisticated madness! Controlling this Hub is tantamount to controlling the galaxy!" Phaleron stomps away from me and stares through the glass of Data Stack B, trying to take deep breaths to calm himself.

In silence, I tread behind him. With the lightness of a feather, I ease my hand onto his tense shoulder. Phaleron's brow wrinkles and his shoulders level. He turns away from the glass. "Can we stop this man, Lincoln? Can we stop those...things?"

"Do you have fire extinguishers?"

"Yes, of course." Phaleron smirks.

"Good. The Dagerites are relentless but not invincible. I'm convinced they are susceptible to the extremes of cold and fire."

"Fire extinguishers?" A stern voice reverberates off the sparse walls behind me.

Spinning toward the source of the complaint, I nearly smack into the security detail's section chief. His dark verdant skin-tone radiates with his incredulity. "You can't be serious? Let me contact mobile security and find out how far along they are in breaching the entrance."

I take a glance at the name on the patch on his jacket. "Like I said, Chief Jazonis is it? This technique worked earlier. And with what I've witnessed of Lt. Lincoln's increasing abilities, you don't have time to wait for backup."

Jazonis' glare burns right through me as he rests his hand on his holstered gun. "My team is supposed to go in there and defend themselves against a techno-organic threat with only fire extinguishers?"

Great, this Jazonis fellow is cut from the same combat-fatigued cloth as Alvarez.

"Listen, not only have I seen it work," I try to say with authority. "But you know better than me, firing your gun will be problematic if we have to go into the more sensitive areas of this data stack."

Phaleron raises his eyebrows and lunges forward. "I'm sorry, Chief Jazonis, but the ambassador is correct. You know we cannot have any weapons fired inside the data stack, especially inside the clean room vault."

The air goes out of Jazonis' chest. "Fine. My team will...re-equip."

Phaleron pats Jazonis on his back to reassure him of my plan. But is it enough to go into the data stack, armed with only fire extinguishers on my say so alone?

Pushing the doubt from my mind, I turn to Gen. Alvarez who is checking his borrowed rifle. "General, you need to put that pea-shooter away and arm yourself with an extinguisher. Outfit everyone."

Before he speaks, Alvarez stares at me like he is examining me for deadly Subian eye-worms. "Ambassador, I'm gonna keep my *pea-shooter*, thank you very much, but after what I've seen today, carrying an extinguisher can't hurt I suppose."

"What?" he asks. My surprise at Alvarez actually listening to my advice must show on my face. "I might be an asshole, Ambassador, but I'm not stupid."

He spins away from me around to Sgt. Jones. "Sergeant, take five of these men and get as many extinguishers as you can carry."

"Yes, sir!" Jones salutes, practically skipping down the hallway with five security guards on her six.

The air of ex-military hangs over the guards like a flag-draped coffin. The way they hop-to, fall in line, and carry themselves, that unmistakable swagger screams military discipline. It's probably why they follow Alvarez' orders so readily.

"Ambassador." Phaleron calls me over. "There is a cyber-security station on this floor I need to get to. From there, I can regulate the temperature control system and activate the sprinkler system to spray the cold fire repellent. I'll also need to strengthen the computer system's firewalls. That might keep the Dagerite programming out."

"The Dagerites were created to bust through most firewalls, you know."

"If worse comes to worst," Phaleron explains. "I will save the contents of our data stacks as SR codes burned onto analog film and transfer them to our off-site polar location. But it's going to take time since my chief archivist is missing. It will be only myself coding."

"My assistant, Atia Watkins, can lend a hand at shoring up your digital defenses." I wave her over. She had been salivating at the advanced computer technology beyond the glass doors of Data Stack B.

"In a pinch," I say, presenting her to Phaleron. "She can act as your chief archivist. She's an expert hacker."

"Whoa, whoa!" Atia marches over, shaking her head. "I code, Mr. Phaleron! I don't hack! I code! Really, Ambassador?"

I give Atia a sly wink. "Keep in contact with me on your mobile."

My young assistant sucks her teeth at me in mock defiance, but quickly obliges, taking out her mobile. She removes a wireless earbud and places it into her ear. I do the same with my mobile.

"Come this way. Miss Atia, is it?" Phaleron guides her by the arm. The two speed past the elevators down the hall from where we originally came from.

Sgt. Jones and the other security guards return with state-of-the-art fire extinguishers. Their canisters and triggers are more elaborate than anything I've seen in your typical office building. Sgt. Jones presents them to Gen. Alvarez.

He pumps his fist into the air in quick jabs. "Outstanding, Sergeant! Is there enough for everyone?"

"Yes, sir. And a few extra just in case."

I reach for one of the extras.

"What do you think you're—? " Alvarez starts in on me but pauses. "You know what, Ambassador? Go right ahead. Take one. I haven't been able to stop you folks from getting in the way since this little class trip from Hell started. Why would you stay out of the way now?"

Picking up the extra extinguisher, I simply shrug and remain silent. The weight of the large, metal cylinder comes as a rude awakening. Wielding one of these things offensively won't be easy. Fukuwara snatches up an extinguisher as well, showing no ill-effects from its weight. The scowl on his face dares anyone to try and stop him.

"I'll take one too." Rebecca says, weighed down by an extinguisher she hoists at an awkward angle.

Like Alvarez did to me, I want to admonish her. But like Alvarez, I think better of it. No sense being a hypocrite.

Chapter Eight

Upon our approach to the glass doors of Data Stack B, Security Chief Jazonis takes point. He stops, then turns, standing resolute.

"Our target is Lt. James Lincoln. The belief is he intends to infect Data Stack B's primary server stack. That would likely place the subject at the rear, close to the vault door of the Clean Room. Since security protocols have been activated, the vault door should now be locked down. The only way that door is opening is if Archive Master Phaleron deactivates it. We'll probably meet resistance there. Under no circumstances is your service weapon your primary option, especially if Lincoln manages to get into the Clean Room. If you have to use your gun, you better make sure it's at point-blank range and you hit the target. If not, you will have me to answer to."

Security Chief Jazonis scans us to see if anyone has any questions. Satisfied there are none, he turns to Alvarez. "General Alvarez, I yield command of the next phase of this operation to you."

Alvarez stands shoulder to shoulder with the lead security guard. He still manages to appear commanding in his uniform jacket over an undershirt. "Thank you, Chief Jazonis. Team, no doubt the subject is trying his damnedest to get into that vault. That is not an option. Quick and silent is the order of the day. Verbalize only when identifying the subject. Buddy up into teams of two; one uses their extinguishers to contain and the other takes down the subject with heavy spray. And to reiterate what Chief Jazonis said, try not to use your guns inside there. We cannot afford to cause damage in the Data Stack with errant shots. If after all of your best efforts have been exhausted and he still resists, fall back and give someone else a chance. Understood?"

"Sir, yes sir!" Sgt. Jones shouts, being the only real grunt present. A look of regret swiftly spreads across her face when she realizes the guards acknowledge the general's commands with only simple nods. They do help Jones save face by pretending not to notice her blush.

Alvarez tightens his grip on his extinguisher. "You now know the drill. Let's move out. Oh yeah, Ambassador Dylan, Deputy Secretary French — Try not to get us killed in there."

While Rebecca shakes her head in disgust, I tell him we'll try, stretching out each word with disdain.

"Master Phaleron, have you deactivated the lock on Data Stack B yet?" Jazonis asks while pressing a button on his jawbone comms. He listens for a few seconds. "Good. Roger that, sir."

The security leader places his palm onto a gray pad on the door. After a green light scans his handprint, the magnetic locks disengage with a soft buzz and a clunk. The door slides open, releasing a rush of cool air. With his head on a swivel, the security chief and another guard advance. Fukuwara anxiously follows beside a guard he has partnered with. After a couple of guards enter together, Alvarez and his security partner step slowly inside. A Sunderian guard leads Rebecca and myself inside Data Stack B's monitoring area. My palms sweat so bad the extinguisher comes close to slipping from my grasp.

The remainder of the security team, four more guards, enter as Sgt. Jones brings up the rear solo.

The outer room of Data Stack B is bathed in a pale blue light. From the corner of my eye, Rebecca shivers as the considerable cool permeates the environs in order to prevent the massive amount of computer hardware from overheating. Four monitoring stations, two on either side of the main aisle, are absent of their personnel. But a few meters beyond the monitoring station on the far left, I am soon proven wrong.

"Over here." An Earther guard speaks at a conversational level. With his extinguisher, he gestures toward the body of a male technician sprawled on his back. He wears the blue sash of a chief archivist.

No one else ventures closer to examine Chief Archivist Barrera's body, because the cause of death is obvious. The poor man's neck is broken, his head twisted at an odd angle. Lincoln is getting physically stronger and more violent. If we have any chance, we need to not spook him and hopefully get the drop on *him*.

Since there is nothing more to be done for the chief archivist, the security chief motions us onward. Venturing deeper into the interior of the monitoring room, we stalk our prey. Or are we the ones being stalked? The climate may be cool inside Data Stack B, but defiant beads of sweat trickle down my temples.

The main aisle leads to a small, curved tunnel lit by floor strips. Forced to walk two across, I am fortunate Rebecca is buddied up with me. At least I'll know where she is when things jump off, because I know they will. The end of the tunnel opens wide into the vault's antechamber. There we find Lincoln, in a squat, struggling to get a handhold of the vault door so he can pry it off its hinges. Thank God he's not that strong — yet.

Alvarez steps next to Jazonis, who is still on point. "Lt. Lincoln, if you're in there somewhere, I'm going to need you to stand down! That's an order!"

Lincoln barely registers our presence as we file into the antechamber. In desperation, he continues to grasp at the vault door. His fingers slip off with every attempt.

Out from the middle of our line, Fukuwara squeezes past those in the front. "Lincoln... — Jimmy... — buddy! What's going on, man? It's me, Kentaro! Kenny!"

While Fukuwara tries to appeal to his friend, I pull out my mobile. Attempting to be surreptitious, I duck behind a burly Earther guard in front of me and connect to Atia. I keep my voice to a whisper. "Atia, we've made contact with Lincoln. How's it going?"

"We're in position," she says. "We're already installing stronger firewalls for the data stack. But Phaleron says it's only a temporary measure depending on how resilient the Dagerites are. We might have to move the data off site. But that takes time. As far as temperature goes, say the word. Master Phaleron is ready to drop it even more."

"How low?"

Atia murmurs something to Phaleron I can't make out, but in a moment she's back. "He's prepared to drop the temperature to 272 Kelvin. Any lower and it may damage the servers."

"Do it."

Atia mumbles once again to Phaleron for a moment before coming back on the line. "The temperature should be dropping noticeably — now."

The high levels of stress burning through us all is revealed by the condensation now flaring from everyone's quick breaths. Good going, Phaleron!

"Jimmy, you need to come with us." Fukuwara continues to hold out hope for his friend. "Man, if you're in there, fight so we can help you."

Lincoln sighs like a child who has been called away from play by his mother. "Jimmy is not home, *Kenny*. And I can help myself, thank you."

Fukuwara takes three quick steps forward. Before he can take a fourth, Lincoln sticks out his arm as if to halt him. From his hand, black Dagerites stream out in a thick metallic rope configuration. In one fluid motion, he swings it like a whip and strikes Fukuwara across the chest. The sickening thwack sounds like he slapped a side of beef. Swept off his feet, Fukuwara bounces against the antechamber wall like a deflated ball. With the wind knocked out of him, the captain clutches his chest in a world of pain.

"Light him up!" Gen. Alvarez barks, being the first one to spray his extinguisher.

Jazonis and another guard on point take a knee and unleash the contents of their extinguishers full force at the co-pilot's face and center mass. Lincoln hisses like an exposed snake, recoiling in distress from the extremely cold foam and gas quickly filling the antechamber and tunnel. Slinking backward into the artificial fog, Lincoln continues to attack. He swings his Dagerite whip arm in wild slashes at anyone within his vicinity. One of the kneeling guards takes a shot to his ribs. He is sent reeling hard into the side of the tunnel. On the return, the whip narrowly misses Jones' head, forcing her to roll to one side. The nanite lash cracks across the back of a guard who fumbles with his extinguisher's trigger. The dark metallic tendril quickly snakes across the floor, taking the legs out from under yet another guard. Stern-faced, Jazonis maintains his position. Either out of courage or foolishness, he steps up, spraying more flame-retardant square into Lincoln's chest. Rocked backward like a man on the edge of a roof, Lincoln forces himself forward, but stumbles and drops to one knee.

Instead of showing discomfort, his face contorts into a pinched visage, as if vexed by our resistance. The Dagerite purpose is to infect and control. Interfering with that directive must not compute.

"Press the advantage!" Alvarez yells moving forward.

Everyone shuffles past the downed guards and Fukuwara. At this point, even I have space enough to spray Lincoln. The nozzle and trigger are freezing to the touch, but I ignore the numbness in my fingers and let loose, helping pin Lincoln against the vault door. His whip stops lashing out. Instead, it quivers as it recedes back into his hand with a sickening slurp. From his other hand pressed against the vault door, he releases a stream of Dagerites into the crease.

"He's found a way in!" I yell at my mobile. "Phaleron, open the door!"

Atia comes on the line with Phaleron conferenced in a split screen. "Are you crazy, Boss? He'll get into the server vault!"

"He's already *in* the server vault! They're small enough to get in through the crease! And don't call me 'Boss'!" I switch my mobile to a single screen of the Master Archivist. "Phaleron, you have to open the vault door. We have to stop this from the inside now!"

Phaleron thinks for an extended split second, swallows hard and types a command into his console. "Vault door opening, Ambassador!"

The vault door rolls open, exposing an enormous circular column of servers stacked several stories high. A thick rush of even colder air spills out, making the tunnel almost unbearable. Weakened, Lincoln staggers back into the vault losing his footing. Streams of Dagerites ooze from his hands and flow further inside.

"Move it people!" Alvarez shouts, giving chase along with Jones and the able-bodied guards. I follow as well.

"Rebecca, please stay with the injured," I say turning back toward her.

Rebecca's lithe form lurches forward wanting to follow, but she halts in her tracks. Wild-eyed, chest heaving, and sweat dotting her brow, she collects her thoughts for a second. "Stop those things, Dylan! Stop them!"

Fully expecting to get push-back from her, I'm amazed I do not. Instead, she bends down to check on Fukuwara, who's rubbing his bruised chest. His every breath, raspy sucking gulps. Maybe the madness of the day finally has gotten to the Deputy Secretary. A man has just lashed out at us with a whip composed of nanites, which he shot out from his hand, for God's Sake! We have been on an adrenaline high for who knows how long and maybe Rebecca is finally crashing. She has every right to. I should be crashing too. But five years ago, I believed passing the buck was enough. No, the Dagerites are my responsibility to see through to the bitter end.

Surrounded by guards, Lincoln remains determined. He struggles crawling forward. Dagerites continue to ooze from his hands in a direct line toward the stack.

"I'll cover him!" I point my extinguisher point blank at Lincoln, hitting him with short bursts of cold retardant.

"I can't believe I'm saying this!" Alvarez motions everyone forward. "But you heard the ambassador! He's got this!"

The general waves his extinguisher at the guards, motioning them to set up a skirmish line two meters in front of the stack. The security team obeys, rushing past the slowing stream of Dagerites, forming a humanoid wall. The mechanical bugs are not swayed. Single-minded, they continue their march toward the stack like ants toward a picnic basket. But as they get close, the team sprays without mercy.

Gen. Alvarez pokes out his chin in satisfaction. "That's it, freeze the hell out of them!"

I turn away from Lincoln, who lies on his stomach, gaunt and weak.

Like rats in a trap, the Dagerite line screeches in our eardrums as the security team finishes them off. The metallic thread convulses from side to side like a dying worm. In seconds, the Dagerites desiccate into gray ash. My shoulders slump and I let out a huge sigh of relief, watching these minuscule bastards release their last bit of so-called life.

Ideas on what to do with Lincoln next bombard my mind. He needs to be shackled and quarantined right —.

A sudden stabbing pain lances through the back of my right hand and the meaty pad of my palm. At the point of pain, a bite-mark, a human bite-mark. Lincoln bit me! Like a dumb, rabid dog, he bit me!

I lose my grip on the extinguisher, dropping it, and shuffle away from the lieutenant's emaciated form. He is on his knees with my blood and an expression full of hate smeared across his lips. A loud bang echoes from a direction I can't determine. And now it's Lincoln's blood splattered on my pants leg and blazer from a hole underneath his left eye. The eye rolls down toward the wound directly underneath as the right eye rolls back into his head. For several seconds, his body remains kneeling, as if suspended from invisible strings held by an unseen puppet-master. In an instant, as if someone cut those strings, Lincoln drops backward onto the floor — free.

Chapter Nine

Security Chief Jazonis glares at Sgt. Jones, who continues to point her smoking service pistol out in front of her. "What the —?" He sputters. "Hold your fire, damn it! You could've hit the data stack!"

Jones, calm as a frozen lake in the middle of an Orutan winter, maintains her position. "I'm a pretty good shot," she states, curling her upper lip at the stilled body of Lt. James Lincoln. She looks ready to plug him as many more times as need be.

"Ambassador, are you alright?" Gen. Alvarez asks me. His voice sounds muffled and far away.

Trying to find the words, my tongue flops around heavy in my mouth. "I...I... I," is all I can spit out. I'm transfixed by my wounded hand. Several of Lincoln's teeth dug deep and broke skin. A perfect oval-shaped bite mark oozes blood, fire-engine red. It flows down my thumb and index finger, steady and thick. The wound burns instead of stings the way a human bite should. Not like I'm overly experienced in the ways of human mastication. When I try to examine the wound closer, a rush of heat flows over me and the world around me slowly falls away. I *observe* the wound, as if outside of myself, fascinated like some gawker eying someone else's injury.

Minute black dots move in, out and around my wound. They repair my damaged hand even as I sense them appropriate the iron in my blood to replicate themselves and spread throughout my bloodstream. It's unlike any feeling of pins and needles I've ever experienced. Tiny champagne bubbles burst in my veins and in my flesh. Effervescent tremors from techno-organic micro-machinery rack my body as the Dagerites begin their invasive sojourn up my arm. Their mission: ride my heartbeat all the way to my brain and erase me!

My breaths come quick, shallow and raspy. My sight has become clouded, and I can't blink. I want to squeeze my eyes shut and will away the sound of my heart pounding in my ears. The extreme whiteness of the Clean Room deceives me. The walls close in and I can't tell where they end, and the floor begins. My legs weaken and the room goes into spin cycle mode. The sound of fearful moaning in the distance bowls toward me like a roiling tide. I strive to identify the source, craving for whoever it is whimpering to be quiet and let me think. But the moaning won't stop - because the moans are mine.

Rebecca rushes into the server vault, frantic. She yells at me. Shakes me. But it's like she does this to someone else in the room. Something wants me to ignore her, to stay calm. Makes sense since there is still work to do. What this *work* is I am unsure of. Something about the server stack. Something about touching it. Something about infection.

Someone else is shouting now. They are blurry. Voice muffled. Oh, it's Fukuwara, rushing into the server vault, calling out Lincoln's name. When he sees Lincoln on the floor dead, with a neat, still smoldering bullet-hole in his left cheekbone, he breaks down. An odd sense of loss washes over me too, but not in the mournful way that would cause an ache in my chest, like when my parents died. Instead, I want to kick and scream like a spoiled child.

****

{Lincoln! No! Damn it! Lost a perfectly good host!}

Wait a second. Who lost a perfectly good host? What host? Who, Lincoln? What a bizarre thought!

{Bizarre thought? Hah! You! You cost me a perfectly good host.}

Why would I think that?

{You didn't. I thought it — for you.}

What? This tone. Different from mine. Brusque. Confident. Invading my consciousness. Kicking down doors.

{It's me.}

But it's not me. Who's me? Why does the answer — linger, no scratches — at the back of my mind?

{Hello there, Ambassador Dylan. You are experiencing the thoughts of me, Tenley Braga, Founder and CEO of Braga Industries. You should feel proud to have a great man, such as myself, inside your head. Now how's about you be a good little drone and shut up those annoying little thoughts of yours and let my Dagerites populate your brain. I need to salvage this situation.}

Ha! I'm hearing things. Tenley Braga inside my head? Definitely not a pleasure to have the likes of such a man as a hallucination.

{That's too bad, Ambassador. I guess the pleasure is all mine then. Do you know what's not a pleasure for me? The fact your two pilots had to be so good at their jobs. Major Gravely would have survived the crash due to my conditioning. But the rest of you people should have done me the favor and died on that shuttle!}

Are the Dagerites beginning to overwrite my mind with their programming? The infection must be causing these delusions. This must be how the symptoms start. Why else would one of the richest men on Earth, be in my mind?

94

{A delusion, sure that's it, Ambassador. If that's what it takes for you to stop resisting, then yes, I'm a delusion.}

If this is a delusion, then I can't give in. I won't. Must get to a medic.

{Go ahead. Be my guest.}

How long until total infection? An hour? Minutes? Seconds?

{Listen, we're almost out of time, Ambassador. The Dagerites have surrounded your cerebral cortex and have begun switching over your motor functions to me.}

What the —? My legs! Moving. On their own. This is no delusion.

{I told you.}

So cold, rattling me to the bone.

{That's the temperature controls of this building and it will destroy my Dagerites soon. You need to move quick, DeMarco.}

If there is one person on Earth and Sunder who could benefit from both the deaths of the Earth-Gov delegation and a takeover of the Archive Tower, that person would be someone like you, Tenley Braga.

{Not bad! I've heard you were a quick study. But I'm so much smarter than you. I'm like...really smart.}

Storm clouds in my head. Dark, heavy, swirling. Thoughts jab, furious, chaotic. Not my own. Can't focus. Outside, the world floats formless. Lightning strikes at my mind's center, pushing me to obey. No! Pain!

{That's what happens to your mind when you resist. You need to stop this pointless defiance, DeMarco. May I call you DeMarco?}

I — I — I...

{DeMarco, I know what you're thinking, and yes, it does make sense that it would be me doing all of this. If you took the time to think about it, sure. When President Rebmann announced the date for the peace talks, my brand lost 30% market share! That was unfortunate...for you and your friends, that is.}

Must warn the others Braga is here, within me.

{You see, DeMarco, Braga Works, Braga Direct, Braga Systems, Braga Soft, Braga Craft, Braga Ideaworks, Braga Research, Techno Braga, even Braga Builder are all heavily leveraged with Earth-Gov defense contracts. The war-show simply must go on!}

What are we in a conference room meeting? Are you trying to sell me your latest business venture? Well, I ain't buying.

{That's too bad. By the way, there's a few Adamahn contracts through some shell corporations floating around out there too! Apparently, that's considered treason, so no one's supposed to know about those. Let's keep that one between us.}

Damn you Braga! Your mind — like a weight — inside mine. Like two fists — pounding on my brain.

{Bet it's unlike any migraine you've ever experienced.}

Get out of my head!

{You're a feisty one! You should be proud to assume a huge role in my latest business venture. The greatest yet. By the way, DeMarco, just so you know, Sunder's Archive complex is in the way of my newest venture: Cloud Braga! Soon, my name will be ubiquitous when it comes to data and cloud storage. And the key to my renewed success will be my secret Dagerites, microscopic employees of the soon to be revealed Nano Braga division! For that, I have you to thank. A sizable political action contribution from me to your second senatorial campaign got me first in line to receive the gift of a defense contract that included ownership of the Dagerites. How I just love our anonymous super p.a.c. laws!}

Why are you telling me all of this?

{Ah, the old 'villain reveals his plan' cliché. It's not that. Full disclosure...I've discovered the infected are more pliable when we are on the same page. In other words, with you now knowing my plan, it makes it easier for you to accept my instructions. My goals become your goals.}

****

Braga spits out a laugh that echoes around inside my skull like the braying of an untamed horse. My body seizes, first my left arm, next my right leg, followed by my left foot. He hooks into my motor functions, axion by axion. Each synaptic conquest fires off like the worst migraine combined with the whack of a claw-toothed hammer. I must look a sight to everyone inside the server room, stumbling about, grabbing wildly at my head in a pathetic attempt to push Braga out.

"Dylan, are you okay?" Rebecca asks me over and over from what sounds like many kilometers away.

I want to respond. I want to tell her. I want to tell them all Tenley Braga is behind today's mayhem. Instead, only painful grunts and excruciating moans come out of my mouth.

****

Let me speak, damn it!

{No, DeMarco! If necessary, I will do the speaking. Just give in to the inevitable.}

Never! Won't let you re-write me or control me!

{Go to the server stack, DeMarco! Now!}

****

Braga's commands come with more force and pain behind them. But I push back. The storm in my mind swirls in the opposite direction for a brief moment. As long as a spark of resistance burns within me, he can send as much pain as he likes.

{Go to the server stack, DeMarco! Touch it! Just touch it! I'll take care

of the rest.}

Braga attempts to cajole me, and my legs take two wobbly steps toward the data stack. I fight off the command and take one wobbly step backward. Once again, I try to speak, but I'm cut short. A wincing pain slashes across one hemisphere of my brain to the other, doubling me over. I hear myself scream. Sweat pours from my face.

{Damn it, DeMarco! Why so willful? How's about I send more Dagerites to overwhelm your cerebrum and shut that willpower down?}

Braga's anger heats hot within my head. He grabs at my mind with invisible hands. Imaginary fingers prod and poke at the ridges of my brain. But there is something to be said about consciousness; it's a slippery thing.

****

{Why aren't you mine already, DeMarco? For all intents and purposes, I am you now! Gravely and Lincoln didn't put up this much fuss. What's with you? I am you, DeMarco Dylan! I am you!}

Are you sure, Braga? Are you me now? I still feel and think — like me.

****

Not sure if the rest of the room agrees. Everyone surrounds me in a circle of fear. The guards hold their extinguishers halfway, unsure if they should spray me. Gen. Alvarez' jaw is on the floor while his right eyebrow twitches toward the ceiling. Sgt. Jones has a definite idea about what to do next written all over her face. She has raised her service weapon again, pointing it right at my face.

"No! Wait!" Rebecca screams. She slides between us.

Jones grips the gun tight with both hands, one eye is closed to perfect her shot. "Stand down, Deputy Secretary."

Rebecca moves in sync with Jones, who tries to slip around her. "Stop, Jones! Please, that's Ambassador Dylan!"

"That is no longer the ambassador, ma'am. Let me finish this." Jones' attempts to sidestep Rebecca are impeded once again. Together they are locked in a *danse macabre* over my continued existence.

{We've lost the element of surprise, DeMarco! For that you have to pay!}

Braga's rages mean more pain. The wound in my hand hurts tenfold, dropping me to my knees. Grabbing my wrist, I grit my teeth and try to push through the agony. A second wave of pain erupts throughout my hand and up my arm, dropping me on my seat. In an attempt to regain some measure of myself, I fumble at my belt buckle and manage to pull it off. With some difficulty, I make a tourniquet in hopes to stave off Braga's control.

{Go ahead. Tie off the hand, DeMarco. It won't stop me. The Dagerites are having their way in your bloodstream, using the iron to replicate themselves. They're already in your brain. In time, you'll be mine — fully!}

Braga sounds so nonchalant as if everything he's planned is inevitable. A part of me wonders though. *He said he was me.* Braga relishes the chance to answer.

****

{Yes, I am you. And together we'll kill all these pesky insects in this room as our/my/your first order of business.}

I won't let you.

{Next, we'll infect this data server stack and spread out to the other data centers in the Archive complex. From there we'll fan out to every computer system and cloud service in the galaxy. With the Sunder Archive compromised, every sentient being will come to Cloud Braga for their

information storage. We will control everyone by controlling their data; their very secrets will be mine. We will be the masters of all data. Who could stop us? We'll be in every defense network, every company and every home. You can't ask for more power than that.}

****

The pain in my hand increases. But if I am feeling pain that means I am still in control. I just need to focus. With my good hand, I push myself up onto one knee. After a few deep breaths, I raise up on both feet. Jones takes another attempt at a clean shot at me with a quick feint. Rebecca refuses to fall for it and slides into position as my shield.

Braga continues to flash the image of the server stack over and over through the storm within my mind. To keep some semblance of control, I compartmentalize it. Store it off to a recessed corner of my mind. I visualize hiding it behind a vault door similar to the real one for this room.

{Come on, DeMarco. What are you doing? I don't have all day. Go to the server stack!}

I ignore the images. Now I need to withdraw from the outside world, block it all out and go — inside. Must remain calm. Take deep steady breaths. Slow it all down, my mind *and* the outside world. Close my eyes, try to imagine nothing. The afterimage of my surroundings, I push it out. The wild events of the day, I push them out. This utilitarian facility here in Ananda City, I push it out. Rebecca's pained expression, I push it out. My mind must become calm, like the Nighttime Sea on Invictus Two. Deep inhale. Long exhale. The maelstrom in my mind subsides. There is only blackness now and I dive into its center. Braga's mind is in the void. I sense it. I reach out to him with a question that surrounds him from all angles.

100

****

You say you are me, Braga?
  {That's correct, By the grace of the Dagerites, we are one.}
  How spiritual.
  {I've been practicing for my supporters of faith. Now let me in, DeMarco!
Body and Soul!}

****

The edges of Braga's thoughts are frantic and jittery. His Dagerites continue to dig deeper into my brain. One by one, more synapses flip like switches from DeMarco Dylan over to Tenley Braga. Like a rushing river, his mind begins to wash over the parts of my consciousness I've left exposed.

  Braga, understand this: when I let you in, you are me — and I am You!
  At the declaration, Braga's mind tilts out of balance ever so slightly.
  {I told you that already — Wait! What do you mean?}
  Not waiting for him to flip all the switches in my mind, I open wide a door for Braga. Light from my exposed consciousness pours out, welcoming Braga in. Gluttonous, he seeks to devour all of my mind at once, falling through the door like a rambunctious farm boy jumping into a haystack. Immediately, my thoughts wrap around his like the tentacles of an Orion Hydra. Braga struggles against me, his thoughts racing, consumed with flight over fight. His thoughts, I easily deflect with images of me grinning with confidence. My hold on Braga tightens, allowing me to divert some of my concentration onto the Dagerites, which are still marching like lemmings into my brain. With

due diligence, they follow a signal that hums like a drumbeat. My will comes out of hiding and follows the drumbeat as well, becoming attuned to the mental signal commanding them. Strong and clear, the signal allows me to trace it back into the ether. Unfettered by any mental blocks or defense systems Braga might have, I ride the carrier wave back to its source: Tenley Braga himself.

Through his greedy eyes, I now see *his* world. He (or is it I?) sit in a dark storage room inside The Braga Building back on Earth. He is hooked to medical machinery while a lone young woman, in chic business attire, monitors his vitals displayed on a holographic screen. On my (I mean) his head, is an electronic device shaped like a star. The device, which has shifted his comb-over out of place, is connected by cords to a large computer in the corner of the room. In turn, this computer is connected to a large glass tube. Inside the tube are Dagerites. They move together in a swarm, undulating in a shiny black wave. From our (I mean his) thoughts, commands travel to the computer and into these Earth-bound Dagerites. In turn, they pass the command signal to an up-link at Braga Telecomm, which then sends it through our solar system's wormhole gate station. Once on this side of the wormhole, the gate station shoots the Dagerite signal along a tight radio-magnetic communication beam to these distant Dagerites here on Sunder. The entire process takes less than fifteen seconds, but since time is relative it feels almost instantaneous.

"What the hell is happening?" Braga asks aloud. Part of his mind wriggles free of my grasp. I let it. I want him to know my will is stronger and I control *him*. His potbelly jiggles as his frantic gaze scans around the room.

"Daddy, are you okay?" The pretty young woman asks. She looks more comfortable on a fashion runway than playing nursemaid to a megalomaniac.

102

"My mind, Buffy, he's in my mind!" Braga thinks about reaching for the headgear, but I lower his arms back down and pin them to the chair's armrests.

"Who Daddy?" The fake blond rushes over and leans in real close to Braga's face.

"It's Ambassador Dylan, you stupid cow!"

I let Braga have a modicum of control over his famously big mouth while projecting some choice words about him at the forefront of his thoughts.

"Dylan is in *my* mind!"

"Let me get you out of that thing!" Buffy says while reaching for the headgear, tussling the meager strands of his red-dyed comb-over.

Using Braga's hands, I shove the trust fund baby hard right above her silicone-enhanced chest. Stumbling backward, she lands right on her Betelgeusian butt-lifted ass.

"Daddy, what are you doing?"

"I'm sorry, honey! It's not me." Braga squeezes the apology out in a high-pitched whine usually not heard in his bellicose campaign speeches. "Damn you, Dylan! Get out of my head!"

I overwhelm Braga with one thought: *Let's see how you like it!*

Grabbing control of his fist, I punch him in the face as hard as one can to oneself.

"Ow!" Braga cries out like a child. Blood begins to trickle from his large nose. "You know I can still make you feel pain, Dylan!"

He's right. Back in the server room, the Dagerites have collected in my wounded hand and attack it with fury, stabbing me with a thousand tiny pitchforks.

"Rebecca," I call out, finally regaining much of my vocal function although the pain refuses to let up.

She leans into me, gazing directly into my eyes, trusting that I am still myself.

"I need a huge favor from you," I say, ignoring the pain in my hand. "And it's not going to be pretty."

"Wh-wh-what do you need?" Though she struggles with her words, this does not prevent her eyes from staying locked onto mine.

"I need you to cut off my hand."

Rebecca pauses as the words take time to sink in. When they finally do, her face shatters. "What? That's insane!"

Gen. Alvarez steps next to Jones who still has her gun trained in my general direction. "What a FUBAR thing to ask! How do we know that's you talking in there, Dylan?"

"It's really me, General, I swear it, but I don't know for how long. There are Dagerites in my brain. I can feel them — multiplying."

"I'm not sure I believe you," The general says, giving Jones' pistol a quick glance. "Are you sure it's not the controller controlling *you* right now?"

"That's why I need Rebecca to do what I ask." I turn to her, eyes pleading.

Alvarez presses on. "We should just light you up with cold."

"I would advise against it," I say. "It might cause a negative reaction with the Dagerites."

"Says you or whoever." Alvarez points a meaty digit at me.

"I think I would lose all control. The Dagerites in my hand would lash out like Lincoln did before you had the chance to attack."

Sgt. Jones grips her pistol even tighter and peers around Rebecca. "I'm ready."

"No guns, damn it!" Security Chief Jazonis barks. Jones ignores him, focusing solely on me.

I shake my head. "These things are getting faster. No telling how many of you I'd hurt. The controller is learning."

104

"Who is the controller?" Alvarez asks shaking his fist.

"He won't let me tell. Whenever I try, he associates my speech with my pain centers. But you'd recognize him."

Braga calls out to me. His nasal tenor babbles over and over, but I ignore him.

I turn to Rebecca once again. "Please."

She takes a step back. "Why me?"

The incessant pain makes me dizzy, but I manage to speak. "Five years ago, people believed *my* subcommittee rid the galaxy of the Dagerites. Didn't keep my eye on the ball. Stupid hubris. Too busy looking for political donations and political expedience. Figured I'd kill two birds with one stone by leaving it to the private sector to clean up the government's mess. Thought I'd wash my hands of it all. Didn't follow up with who we dished out the contracts to. Can't afford those mistakes this time."

Rebecca's brow goes slack, her eyes soften. "Dylan, anyone would've done what you did."

A deep sigh escapes from my chest. "I know it could've been anyone, but that *anyone* was me."

Rebecca gives me a mournful look and places her hand on my shoulder. "You're one of the smartest and bravest people I've met in this job, DeMarco."

"And you've never wavered in your belief in my peace proposal, Rebecca, even after all I've revealed to you this day."

Rebecca smiles, her eyes become misty. "Because you are one of the few who believe there was even a peace deal to be made."

"Well, if you still believe in me now, I trust you to do what needs to be done. I'd ask Atia, but she's needed with Phaleron."

Rebecca thinks for a moment and takes a sobering deep breath. She turns back to me with the confidence I'd witnessed back on the shuttle, before the phony turbulence. "Alright. How do you want to do this?"

"There are no knives handy, so we'll use the vault door. Most of the Dagerites have congregated in my hand so I want you to close the door on it. The door is big and heavy enough that it should sever my hand at the wrist. I already have this tourniquet working."

Rebecca's eyes roll at the gory solution I suggest, but she agrees, mustering the necessary amount of conviction without showing any emotion. She walks with me over to the vault's threshold, careful not to touch my arm.

"Boss, don't do this!" Atia's voice comes crackling out of my earbud, which Rebecca now holds. "There's got to be another way!"

"There's no time for another way!" I say. The pain in my hand is so excruciating, I see stars.

Phaleron's voice comes through my mobile. "Ambassador Dylan, I beseech you. You require hospitalization. Amputation via the vault door of the server room? Think of the contamination. This is highly irregular!"

"Master Archivist, this whole day has been highly irregular. Besides, we're running out of time. I have no idea how long I can hold onto the controller and stave off full Dagerite possession."

I lie on the cold floor of the server vault and extend my arm across the threshold at the wrist. My hand, bloody, gashed, and throbbing, is no longer mine to command. So, if thy right hand offends thee, pluck it off, right?

Sgt. Jones whispers to the general, "I have a clear shot, sir."

Alvarez leans over. "Let this play out."

"That control panel over there in the corner should give access to the server stack *and* the vault door," I point.

Rebecca's eyes run up and down the control panel's face. "Shouldn't I need a password or something?"

106

"No," says Phaleron from my mobile. "I've already bypassed the need for credentials and given you control."

Rebecca purses her lips, accepting her responsibility.

"Do you see the door controls?" I ask.

"Yes," she responds in a low monotone, likely steeling herself for what she needs to do.

"I'm ready."

Rebecca locks eyes on me with conviction. I give her no signs of regret. Lowering her head, she presses the app that closes the vault door. Like a mother lulling her child to sleep, the door's mechanism hums with energy. The massive circular portal rolls on its track with minimal effort. The last image I see before I close my eyes is the server stack, proudly rising dozens of stories like a massive Greco-Roman column dedicated to preserving the galaxy's information. All that is left for me to do now is wait.

{This won't keep me out you know!}

As long as I keep my connection to Braga through the Dagerites in my brain, I believe I have a chance to free myself and more. Since the Dagerites couldn't control the dead bodies of Gravely and Lincoln, the pain and shock from the trauma should be enough to kick Braga out of my mind. What's a hand worth these days? The stored information of the entire galaxy?

{You're mad! That's it! You are simply mad!}

Braga thinks he has me figured out.

Sure Braga, go with that. In the meantime, I want you to feel this too.

As I hear the vault door edging closer, I hold tight to Tenley Braga's mind back on Earth. My willpower wraps around his consciousness the way a Ganymedian anaconda grasps its prey and refuses to let go.

{Get out of my mind, DeMarco Dylan! Please!}

Braga's futile thoughts struggle against mine and he screams.

{Buffy, unhook me from this contraption!}

She cannot hear him. I return the favor by mentally constraining his vocal functions, in essence wiring his big mouth shut. Our minds project the image of a brightly lit room, the walls and floors awash in gold. Braga wildly rolls his mind around and around like a trapped Floridian gator in a final attempt to wriggle free.

{No! Please, DeMarco! This is insane! I beg you! I'll pay you anything! Name your price! I'll give you anything! My daughter, Buffy? You can have her! Her husband is a wimp! She's the heir to it all! Don't worry about my sons. All three are morons!}

Braga's rant becomes mere white noise simply blending in with the hum of the vault door. It rolls past my head with a 'shhh' sound, quieting any final misgivings I might have. Soon, that sound is followed by the nauseating squish of flesh and the crunch of bone. For a heartbeat, I feel nothing, only the frigid air conditioning of the server room flowing across my body. As if signaled by some sadistic artillery commander, all the neurons in my wrist fire off at once. There is screaming, Braga on Earth and me on Sunder. I'm unable to distinguish between us. Because the pain is so great, my mind leaves both bodies, I guess to help me cope with the shock. My mind hovers over my form as I experience it as if someone else has had their hand severed. Not me. Foolishly, I shatter the illusion when I open my eyes to the sight of blood spurting out from where my hand used to be. The vision of my wrist spraying blood, like a fountain, is the last thing I see before a veil of darkness drifts over my eyes and mind.

Chapter Ten

Through varying waves of alertness, the world returns to me out of a deep, dark cloud. Muffled sounds follow bright light. My eyes painfully adjust to the brightness. Steadily emerging bits of detail coalesce. It takes me a while to realize where I am. The smell of antiseptic cleanser helps me get my bearings and I see I am lying in a hospital room a few shades whiter than white. The med-bed is comfortable enough considering all I've gone through. My fugue state informs me I'm hopped up on painkillers. For that I am thankful.

"Ah, Ambassador Dylan, you're finally awake!"

I let my head fall to the right and there is a Sundarian nurse in scrubs checking my vitals on a 3-D holograph. "You might feel lightheaded and groggy. That's normal, but please don't try to move too much. Okay?"

Trust me, moving is not in my immediate plans.

Weak, my head falls to the left, only to discover Rebecca curled up in a chair, asleep. She is a welcome sight, sitting sideways, with her legs dangling over the armrest. She is at peace and appears more attractive to me than even our initial meeting on the EEF Concorde. No idea how long she has been there, but she is still wearing the same clothes underneath some hospital scrubs.

"Rebecca." My throat hurts and it is hard to speak.

Rebecca's eyes half open. She rustles around, then stretches. When she notices me looking at her, she perks up and jumps to the side of my bed. "Dylan, you're finally awake!"

"Which hospital —?" My mind races with the slow slog back to consciousness.

Anxious, Rebecca grips the side rail of my bed. "You're in Ananda General Hospital."

"How long was I out?"

"You've been out two days. They tell me you're in good hands. Oh god, I'm sorry. I shouldn't have said *hand*."

"No, it's alright." Underneath the covers, there is a dull ache at the wrist where my right hand should be. "Thank you for...what you did."

"You're welcome, I guess." Rebecca lowers her head, unable to meet my eyes. "But I'm still sorry!"

I caress her smooth hand with my remaining one and a serene smile draws across her round face. Here in the quiet aftermath, Rebecca's hand feels different now. Gone is the cold slick sweat brought on by a day of terror. In its place, an extremity which is soft, fearless and full of warmth. I never want to let go. Her touch stirs me to life.

"Ambassador Dylan." The nurse politely pushes me back down when I struggle to sit up. "You mustn't exert yourself. Rest."

Although I let out a disappointed sigh, I know she's right. Just that little bit of movement tires me, but I still need to know how we fared back in Data Stack B. "Tell me we stopped the Dagerites."

Rebecca takes a moment as if she's trying to find the right words and purses her lips. "We did. The server stack is safe. Data Stack B is safe. The Archive Tower is safe. Master Phaleron has everything under control. He's in the midst of performing a full system scan of the entire Archive to make sure things are fine."

The way she speaks, slowly, it's obvious Rebecca is holding back some bad news.

"And what about Tenley Braga? Did the authorities get him?" I ask.

"Huh?"

"Tenley Braga." I repeat the businessman's name with a minute level of pride, knowing I can finally do so without negative consequence to my pain centers.

"Tenley Braga?" Rebecca still has no clue what I'm talking about. "Why would you ask about him?"

"There's evidence back on Earth his conglomerate is not only the buyer of the Dagerites' original tech firm, but Braga is also behind all that's happened!"

"Are you sure?" Rebecca scratches her head. "That's whose name hurt you so much to say?"

"Yes. Braga himself was behind our assassination attempt, the Archive infection attempt, all of it." I tell this to her, trying to ignore the irritation where my hand used to be. "Our shuttle crashing was objective one. We were right. Maj. Gravely *was* meant to be the sole survivor in order to complete objective two, infecting the Tower."

Rebecca cocks her head. "Really? Tenley Braga got personally involved in all of this? Wow! Explains a lot."

"How so?"

"Braga has been all over the news these last two days, so is our ordeal, but his story is almost eclipsing ours."

"How is Braga eclipsing us? The authorities need to arrest him."

Rebecca rocks back and forth on her heels. "Um, that won't be necessary. Tenley Braga is dead."

"What? How?" Still too weak and groggy, I fail at trying to sit up in my bed.

Rebecca presses a finger to her temple. "He had a massive stroke back on Earth."

"A stroke?" Did I hear her correctly? "I didn't think the shock would be that great. Wow, must have been some feedback loop I gave him."

Rebecca's eyes widen as she brings her hand to her open mouth. "Are you saying you had something to do with his stroke?"

I think for a second. "I guess I had *everything* to do with Braga's stroke."

Rebecca leans over the railing of my med-bed like a stern mother. "And what do you mean by *feedback loops*?"

"If there was anyone ready for Dagerite contamination it was me, I guess. Anyone ever attacked before by those little bastards, had no clue as to what was happening to them. When Lincoln infected me, I was well aware of what was happening. So, I was able to put up enough of a fight and keep them from taking over my mind. It was the toughest fight I've ever experienced."

Rebecca strokes my arm. "I'm sure it was. You were in so much distress and I had no clue how to help."

A cold shudder ripples through my body. "Tenley Braga's voice was in my head the entire time I fought. I must admit, he can be persuasive."

"And Braga controlled the Dagerites directly?" Rebecca stands off to the side dumbfounded.

"Right. From one of his office complexes on Earth, he sent a tight-beam signal to the Dagerites on Sunder and used them to control Maj. Gravely and Lt. Lincoln." Saying their names, I can't help but consider what might have become of me if I was unable to resist.

"Those poor men," Rebecca mutters. "And that's some advanced tight-beam technology he must have there."

"The delay lag had to be in the single digits."

Rebecca looks off into the distance. "Earth-Gov needs to get their hands on that."

How selfishly evil Braga was to use two unsuspecting family men for his grand game. And I was to be the third pawn on his chessboard.

"He kept imploring me to infect the server stack," I confess. "But I refused."

Rebecca gives my arm an encouraging squeeze. "You showed a ton of restraint."

"He controlled the level of pain in my hand, but I used that pain as a way to follow his *signal*, so to speak, back to the source: which was Tenley Braga hiding in a spare storage room in his office building on Earth, hooked up to Dagerite communication tech."

Rebecca's eyes widen. "Reports say his daughter found him collapsed in a hallway near his office."

"Bull! Buffy Braga was right there! I saw her, even pushed her using Tenley's own arms. She's involved up to her Tiffany necklace as well!" I get excited, so the nurse decides to push me back into my pillow again.

"Maybe she dragged him out of that storage room to allay suspicion," I continue more subdued. "You need to have the authorities check out that storage room ASAP. If she hasn't moved things already, you'll find a ton of evidence there like a Dagerite signal rig and a handful of Dagerites. Can't be too easy to remove without someone noticing. Room is located on the 87th floor."

Rebecca's gaze becomes clouded. "Um...How do you know all of this?"

"I entered his mind," I answer with a bit of pride. "He knew what I knew, and I knew what he knew. This created what I consider to be a feedback loop!"

113

There's a twinkle in Rebecca's eye. "Ah, I think I get it now."

"He felt my surface thoughts," I explain through the grogginess. "I opened my mind to him entirely. To do that he needed to open his mind to me."

"Incredible!" Rebecca shakes her head.

"When you cut off — my hand, I wanted to get rid of most of the Dagerites and make that bastard feel my pain. I knew the sudden pain would be a shock to his system, but I hadn't counted on a brain hemorrhage."

A satisfied smirk cuts across Rebecca's face. "And to think, I only wanted to use Braga's purchase of the Dagerite side of Rosenfeld Labs to scandalize him out of the election. Meanwhile, he was hands-on with multiple counts of attempted murder, sabotage, and extortion. I'll advise the president to have Buffy Braga arrested and the family assets frozen. We need to see what else he was hiding before his children get a hold of things and cover up any of the old man's involvement."

"That's a good idea. I'd like to be there when you turn over that rock."

Bouncing on her toes, Rebecca leans closer. "I can't believe how deep his thumbs were shoved into that Dagerite pie! Oh, I'm sorry, Dylan! I did it again. I said *thumbs*."

"It's okay, Rebecca."

The door to the hospital room swings open. A doctor, an older Earther woman, enters. "Ah, you're awake! Good! I'm Dr. Albright and I brought some of your friends!"

Albright is followed in by Atia, Cory Murray, Sgt. Jones and Gen. Alvarez. She takes out her medical analyzer, a small cylindrical piece of shiny metal with small buttons on the surface, runs it over my body and compares the readouts on the med-bed monitor.

Atia lunges over the side rails of the med-bed, holding a knapsack and gives me a tearful hug. "I'm so glad you're you, Boss!"

"I'm glad I'm me too and don't call me 'Boss.'" I wriggle around so I'm not asphyxiated by her embrace. "Atia, you and Master Phaleron did good work back there."

Atia sits in the chair Rebecca had slept in, beaming an appreciative yet humble smile. "Deputy Secretary, I've got that change of clothes you wanted." Atia offers the knapsack to Rebecca, who puts both hands over her heart in appreciation.

Cory approaches and pats my leg with his good hand. His broken arm is immersed in a bright blue liquid nutrient-bath splint and sling contraption. "I heard you were awesome out there, Sir. You solved it all!"

"Everybody did their part, Cory. How's the arm?"

"It's coming along nicely, Sir." He raises his arm a smidgen. "Dr. Albright says to give it a few more days and I'll be signing visas again in no time."

Sgt. Jones steps up next. She doesn't smile, but her eyes are bright and friendly. "Sorry I was going to shoot you, Ambassador."

"That's alright, Sergeant." I try to assure her I have no hard feelings with a soft tone. "The entire galaxy was at stake. I wouldn't blame you one bit if you had shot me. But I sure am glad you didn't."

Jones purses her lips, pleased all has been forgiven. "I swear to you it would've been quick and painless." She lowers her eyes and backs away, holding up the wall with her straight posture.

Now it is Gen. Alvarez' turn. He saunters forward lacking his usual bluster, but still maintaining a certain level of pomp. "Ambassador Dylan, your actions and intuition during this operation were simply outstanding. Your sacrifice will be appreciated and honored for years to come. That's why I'm recommending an award ceremony for you. Real 'medal of honor' type stuff. Whatever it is you civilians get."

My heart warms in my chest and my eyes mist over. "Why, you shouldn't have. Thank you very much, General. I do not know what to say."

Alvarez leans in close as if he doesn't want the others to hear. "May I be honest? I haven't had this much fun since this police action I was involved in back on Izo Huen."

"What happened on Izo Huen?" Rebecca asks.

"That's classified, Ma'am." Alvarez quickly backs away from the med-bed.

Rebecca grins and rolls her eyes. "Of course it is."

I notice someone is missing from my coming out party. "Where's Captain Fukuwara?"

General Alvarez suddenly stands at attention. "Capt. Fukuwara volunteered to accompany Lt. Lincoln's remains back home to his family on Earth."

"But what about the infection?" I ask.

Gen. Alvarez folds his arms. "I gave orders for the hospital's Haz-Mat unit to perform full decontamination protocols."

Dr. Albright clasps her arms behind her back. "Your orders were carried out to the letter, General. Both Lt. Lincoln and Maj. Gravely's bodies were cremated. There was no trace of active nanites."

Everyone becomes silent and pensive for several moments. An icy chill runs through my prone body.

For a closer look at me, Dr. Albright squeezes past a somber Gen. Alvarez and breaks the silence. "Tell me Ambassador, how does the hand feel?"

"What? How does my hand feel?" I hold up my left hand for her to examine. "It feels fine, Doctor."

"No, no, no." Albright shakes her head. "Your other hand."

What in the galaxy is this quack getting at? Does she have some sort of sick sense of humor?

"What do you mean my other hand, Doctor? It doesn't *feel* at all. The hand is back in Data Stack B. It is gone! There's a dull ache where it used to be, but I'll chalk that up to phantom limb pain!"

Albright ignores my condescension and pats my right arm which has been under the covers since I awoke. "Let's take a look at your hand, Ambassador."

I cannot bear to look at my stump yet. But like pulling a bandage off a scab, I decide to get it over with. I do the doctor's bidding and pull my arm out from under the covers. There is a loud gasp, then everyone in the room remains silent. I gasp in shock at the sight before me. My eyes behold *my hand,* but my mind refuses to understand what it is I'm seeing. Where my right hand once was and what should have been a surgically mended stump, there is an all-black, metallic, lustrous, constantly undulating hand. Dagerites.

Deep furrows digging into the palm mirror the same lines that criss-cross my left hand. Smaller grooves copy the fingerprints found on its fleshy counterpart. Movement just underneath the surface sends a sensation up my arm like a mix of pins, needles, and fizzy soda.

Upon initial inspection, I believe Dr. Albright has fashioned me a state-of-the-art prosthetic. But no one makes prosthetics like this unless they are skilled in using the Dagerites. I am certain that person and skill set does not exist, yet.

"What the hell is going on here?" I sputter. The sight of my Dagerite-composed hand makes me cringe. As the fingers ripple and the palm vibrates; it all manages to stay connected to my wrist.

"Please try to remain calm, Ambassador." Albright's attempt at bedside manner falls on deaf ears. "We tried to remove the nanite infection from your body without killing you, but the Dagerites proved resistant to all current forms of treatment. We scanned your brain and found nanite clusters in the areas controlling motor function and cellular regeneration. You lost so much blood, not just from the amputation, but from the nanites using the iron in your blood to replicate themselves. Surprisingly, that process quickly stabilized. Then I learned, from your colleagues, the purpose of these nanites, and examined their behavior. They're not *hacking you*, as young Miss Atia put it. Instead, they appear to be fully integrated into your nervous system. They're working *with* you!"

"Working with me?" Something prickles at the back of my scalp and quivers in my gut.

"Yes," Dr. Albright says, slack mouthed and nodding incessantly. "The Dagerites are working with you in the most symbiotic way possible, as just another extremity. But an extremity with so much potential."

Marveling at my Dagerite hand, I can't help but fear what I may have become. Am I myself or am I now some cybernetic freak? Maybe I'm in control now, but will the Dagerites one day usurp my dominance when I least expect it? If someone else touches my hand, will I infect them? Am I safe to even be around? The doctor believes we are working together in harmony. What if that changes? Maybe it's not a case of 'if' but 'when'?

Pushing the 'what ifs' to the back of my mind, I focus my will on exerting control over my hand. An electric tingle courses from my Dagerite palm into my fingers. The sensation is beyond natural. The undulating motion of the microscopic Dagerites increases with my initial excitement, but for only a moment. Once I calm myself, in an attempt to come to terms with my predicament, the activity within the hand quickly minimizes, leaving a semi-stable fist that looks as if carved from the glossiest of onyx. The dull ache in my wrist serves to remind me of my remaining humanity.

Will I ever be in full control of my person, or must I accept this parasitic partnership for the rest of my life? The question begins to consume me. But when I think *point*, the hand does in fact point. I think *wiggle fingers* and the fingers indeed wiggle. I think *fist* and it makes a fist. It doesn't feel like someone or something else is performing these actions. It feels like me. I point. I wiggle my fingers. I make a fist. As long as I have something to say about it, I am in control.

"That's some upgrade you've got there, Boss." Cory points at my hand with enthusiasm.

"Don't call me 'Boss,' Cory," I say unable to stop staring at my glossy fingernails.

"See, I'm not the only one who says it." Atia pouts, sitting back in the chair like a tattle-telling child.

"Upgrade, huh?" I think out loud. "Not so sure about that. You all knew about this?"

Rebecca places a hand on my shoulder. "Yes...we did."

I attempt to curb my racing thoughts by focusing on my new hand. Examining the back, I'm fascinated by the contrast between its smooth blackness next to the deep brown of my wrist's skin. Flipping my hand over, I slowly run my organic fingers along the artificial lifelines carved into the palm and over the manufactured fingerprints on each fingertip.

"Where are we on the peace talks?" I ask needing to change the subject.

"I've been trying to contact the Adamahn, but they've gone silent. Maybe they *were* in concert with Braga?" Rebecca offers meekly.

"I don't accept that." I sit up way too fast and immediately regret it. A wave of lightheadedness rolls over me. "Keep trying, Rebecca, please."

Rebecca pushes on my chest. "Ambassador, don't concern yourself with the talks. They can hold for a few days. You need to rest."

"Nonsense, I feel fine." I sit up on my elbows with the assistance of my new hand. "How's your man, Stubbs, doing?"

"Ken's doing well, considering." Rebecca smiles with muted confidence. "He's lucky. The bullet missed major organs."

"Mr. Stubbs will be in a healing tank for at least two more days," Dr. Albright states. "Afterward, he should be on his feet and ready for some physical therapy."

I'm relieved to hear Ken's prognosis is good.

Outside of my room, a commotion erupts. Voices full of protest get closer and louder. The door swings open and a nurse backs her way in.

"I'm sorry, Dr. Albright. I couldn't stop them. Th-th-they insist on an audience with the ambassador."

Two beings brush past the overwhelmed nurse and lumber inside. Size is the only thing humanoid about them. Their carapaces of brown and black chitin shine bright in the room's fluorescence. Each being stands impossibly upright on a pair of spindly legs with spiky knee-joints. Their thin feet clatter across the tiled floor like bad tap dancers botching a routine. Set back upon their oblong heads, UV-blocking visors protect compound eyes. To these beings, the pink-tinged sunlight of Sunder is considered harsh. Across their small mandibles, the pair wear masks designed to help them breathe. The Sunderian air is too thin for their respiratory systems to cope unaided. Shovel-like forelimbs on their prothoraxes denote a physiognomy meant for digging through their typically subterranean existence. Long thin arms, covered in different intricate designs, extend from their cylindrical mid-thoraxes. Each design signifies the tribe they belong to. Painted on the horn-like antennae on their heads, assorted color stripes signify rank and status. These are Adamahn.

"Please forgive our intrusion, Doctor." The Adamahn with thick white stripes painted diagonally on his horns and body, signifying royalty, holds up his thorax arms in a show of regal humility.

I bolt upright in my bed. "King Bomir?"

The second Adamahn, who has thinner green stripes of parliamentary significance on his horns and body, shuffles next to the king in a more deliberate ceremonial manner, waving his thorax arms in wide circles. "Allow me to introduce Bomir Groban of Tribe Scaptorini, King of the Adamahn!"

Despite our incredulous stares, everyone manages to give polite, but static, nods or awkward bows.

The second Adamahn continues. "I am Gluk Nurmeen of Tribe Scaptorini, Adamahn Prime Minister." His voice has a hiss-like quality from the inert gases pumped into his mask helping him breathe Sunder's thinner atmosphere.

King Bomir skitters forward around his retreating Prime Minister. "We have come to express our unwavering commitment to the peace process. And to express our deepest sympathies for your losses after this despicable attempt at sabotage. I understand you are Earth-Gov Ambassador DeMarco Dylan."

"Yes," I say hiding my Dagarite hand under the covers. "Yes, I am, Your Majesty."

Gluk Nurmeen's shovel hands flutter at me in admiration. "Our Yellow League agents speak of you with great respect. It is a shame we do not have official diplomatic ties; you and I should have negotiated directly."

"Prime Minister, I'm glad there are Adamahn, like yourselves, who are open to peace and courageous enough to talk."

King Bomir folds his bulky mid-thorax arms. "Ambassador DeMarco Dylan, the time for war is over, especially now since we know both sides have been manipulated by mere greed."

"Both sides?" I shift in my bed to make sure I heard him correctly.

Tapping the tribal design on his mid-thorax, Gluk Nurmeen explains. "We, too, were sabotaged by these Dagerites. One of *our* diplomats, who you were supposed to meet with here in Ananda City, was attacked by these so-called Dagerites in his pod room at the hotel provided for him. During his panic, he stopped the incursion by inadvertently setting fire to the room. The Dagerites were destroyed in the blaze, but our representative was badly burned. By the Song of Our Fathers, he is expected to survive."

In my research of Adamahn society, I had come across the term *By the Song of Our Fathers*. It's an idiomatic term the Adamahn use frequently in their speech, in the same way we say, 'By God.' Adamahn males sing a whole host of ritualistic songs for countless occasions. Mostly, it originated from their sacred mating ritual, in which an Adamahn male sings a song, usually one describing his worthiness, to attract and impress a worthy female.

"That's good to hear," I offer, remembering my hypothesis about the nanites being affected by both temperature extremes. "We stopped our Dagerites with cold. Any idea who unleashed the Dagerites on your end?"

"No." Gluk Nurmeen shakes his sclerotic head. "But our investigation continues."

"We should compare notes," I say. "We have a perpetrator who died during his *apprehension*."

King Bomir shuffles an inch closer to the med-bed. "Who was this perpetrator?"

"I discovered one of our own, an Earther named Tenley Braga, was behind the sabotage, Your Majesty."

Gen. Alvarez squirms at my straightforward revelation. He has to accept we need to be open with the Adamahn in order to gain their trust.

"Tenley Braga?" King Bomir's eyes slide side to side behind his visor. "That bombastic Earth merchant?"

"That's the one, Your Majesty," I say.

"That is most interesting," Gluk Nurmeen muses. "The pod room where the attack was perpetrated on us was in the Braga Suites here in Ananda."

"How convenient," I say. "Besides his attempt to eliminate the competition in the field of data collection and storage, Braga wanted the war to continue so his family could have a continuous revenue stream. And as the next president of Earth-Gov, there would have been no end in sight to either the conflict or his war-profiteering."

King Bomir lets his thorax limbs fall to his sides. "Unfortunately, there are many on both sides who believe war is more profitable than peace."

"We need to change that mindset, Your Majesty." I keep a hopeful tone.

King Bormir raises his small head. "Now we both can sing Braga's sins to heaven. Who will run against your president now?"

"Who knows, Your Majesty? There's this uber-religious reformer who's made some decent showings in some of the primaries."

"Great, out of the frying pan and into the Hellfire," Cory mutters. Atia quickly elbows him.

"By the Song of Our Fathers, you should declare your candidacy." King Bomir suggests, rubbing his thorax tribal tattoo. "Though we may forever be plagued by those who seek to use division for personal gain, it is the eternal vigilance of beings such as yourself that is the only true defense."

My cheeks grow hot. "I'm flattered, Your Majesty, but no thanks. In the meantime, I do agree vigilance by all of us is required."

Rebecca leans into the conversation. "If I may be so bold."

"Ah, Deputy Secretary of State Rebecca French." Gluk Nurmeen acknowledges her rank by holding up his thorax limbs and twirling the shovel-hands of his prothorax limbs. "It is an honor."

"King Bomir, Prime Minister Nurmeen, it's also my honor." Rebecca bows with her hand on her heart. "It's been ten star-date months and the ceasefire has held. Why not make it permanent right here and now, Your Majesty? I know a hospital room might be a little...rough, but Earth-Gov is anxious to get this done." Rebecca shakes her fist at the end for emphasis.

The king responds slowly, causing Gluk Nurmeen to fidget with all four of his hands. Quickly he cuts in. "Let us use the official Accords to settle the details, shall we? This way, the entire galaxy may bear witness to such an historic event in full transparency. It is what His Majesty wishes."

King Bomir raises his thorax arms in agreement. "Prime Minister Nurmeen is correct. We must wait and do this out in the open. Our losses have been excessive, as I am sure yours are as well. Believe me, the Adamahn want peace as much as Earth."

Gen. Alvarez deliberately clears his throat loudly. I give him a dirty look. Luckily, the Adamahn either don't notice or don't understand nuanced human communication. Either way, they don't react to our wordless exchange.

After a few more minutes of mere pleasantries, including individual introductions with each member of my team and the oddball question from either Cory or Atia about Adamahn physiognomy, Dr. Albright recommends I get some rest. Must admit, I am exhausted. So, the Adamahn king and his prime minister bow as they take their leave. My group gives lower bows in return, like I taught them. The sound of the Adamahn skittering sideways out of my hospital room, making sure not to turn their backs to us, can still be heard even after the door has closed. Eventually, the sound of their passing is swallowed up by a whirlwind of royal entourage, security, hospital staff and press trailing after them.

Immediately, each of us in our own impressed way, recount the gesture of peace by the Adamahn's ranking hierarchy. Even Gen. Alvarez speaks positively, his natural state of mistrust paused for the moment.

The ordeal has made me thirsty. So, with my Dagerite hand, I point at the pitcher on the table next to my bed, hoping Rebecca can pour me some water for my parched throat. Before she can react, my index finger stretches out into a long tendril and wraps around the pitcher. The vessel's coldness causes an innate tingle to ride up my finger. My middle finger and thumb stretch out as well, wrapping themselves around a cup placed nearby. With surprising deftness, the tendrils pour out splashes of water, spilling a few drops here and there. Using my elongated middle finger, I bring the cup to my cracked lips. The cool liquid tastes so good in my dry mouth, I decide to savor it before swallowing. Remembering my manners, I offer the pitcher to the group, who with varying degrees of discomfort, politely turn me down.

Embarrassed, I quickly retract the fingers back into a more acceptable length and shape. But Rebecca quickly sweeps up my Dagerite hand and holds it tight in hers. It's such a comfort to be able to feel the confidence in her hand's soothing warmth.

"Oh, it tingles," Rebecca says patting the back of my new hand. She shows no fear or trepidation holding it in hers.

Clasped together, my Dagerites do not attempt to infect her. Our hands mingle in the most natural of ways, like human couples have done since time immemorial. My positive energy passes from my nano-palm into hers, as her positive energy passes into mine.

Rebecca flashes a contented smile, making my body go light and weightless for the first time in weeks. "Holding your hand is going take some getting used to."

I reflect back her smile. "I'm willing to give it some practice if you are."

Acknowledgements

To my writing group, The Climbing Ivies of Blackrock. You have helped me immensely with your thoughtful and skilled critique of this novella. Thank you. I am forever grateful.

To my wife, Rochell, thank you for your unflagging support and understanding whenever I retreated into my writing time.

About the Author

When he's not writing new worlds, Ezekiel Springer Jr., aka "Junior" to his family and "Zeke!" to his friends, edits movies and commercials as a post-production technician for a popular cable network. A New York native and lifelong Mets fan, he lives in the Boogie Down Bronx with his wife and an impressive comic book collection.

Website: https://ezekielspringer.wordpress.com/
  Twitter: @zeke_pen67
  Facebook: https://www.facebook.com/ZekeTheFreak67

www.ingramcontent.com/pod-product-compliance
Lightning Source LLC
Chambersburg PA
CBHW061251170626
46809CB00007B/2951